ADOBE CENTORI

and the

SILVER MEDALLION

Statehood of Affairs Series

Daniel R. Cillis, PhD

ADOBE CENTORI AND THE SILVER MEDALLION
STATEHOOD OF AFFAIRS SERIES

Certain characters in this work are historical figures, and certain events portrayed did take place. However, this is a work of fiction. All of the other characters, names, and events as well as all places, incidents, organizations, and dialogue in this novel are either the products of the author's imagination or are used fictitiously.

iUniverse books may be ordered through booksellers or by contacting:

iUniverse
1663 Liberty Drive
Bloomington, IN 47403
www.iuniverse.com
844-349-9409

ISBN: 978-1-5320-5549-2 (sc)
ISBN: 978-1-5320-5548-5 (e)

Library of Congress Control Number: 2018910316

Print information available on the last page.

iUniverse rev. date: 02/24/2022

CONTENTS

Part Three France

PREFACE

Adobe Centori and the Silver Medallion is the third book in the Statehood of Affairs series. Mad Mady Blaylock, Santa Fe Sharon and Gabriela Zena are back along with new characters.

In *Statehood of Affairs*, set in 1911, Centori plays a key role in New Mexico statehood. The unjust commitment of Mad Mady to the Territorial Insane Asylum reveals a plot to find the missing Revert Document. If the document emerges before Arizona and New Mexico achieve statehood, Mexico could recover the lost territories and change history.

The sequel, *Water Damage*, tells the story of Germany's secret war against the U.S. Massive explosions on Wall Street and in New York Harbor alarm the authorities. Centori joins a team of federal agents to track the saboteurs and stop a major terror attack in America.

In *Adobe Centori and the Silver Medallion*, Centori returns to New Mexico where he confronts another challenge when General Pershing offers an army commission to pursue Pancho Villa into Mexico. Then, a plot twist arises—this time the adventure surrounds the legendary Seven Cities of Cibola. Centori leads a systematic search for the lost Cities of Gold as the Great War in Europe casts a shadow on the United States.

DRAMATIS PERSONAE

Adoloreto "Adobe" Centori—Circle C Ranch owner.

Francisco Griegos—Circle C Foreman

Gabriella Zena—Spiritual object of Centori's affection

Elizabeth "Mad Mady" Blaylock—owner Mad Mady's Saloon, friend of Centori

Justo Calabaza—Santo Domingo Pueblo Leader

Francisco Gonzalo—Rancho de las Aquila, owner

Santa Fe Sharon—Mady's sister, co-conspirator

Carmencita—Queen of Mad Mady's Doves, co-conspirator

Carlene Cortina—Airmail and Barnstorming pilot

Raphael—co-conspirator, subservient to Carmencita

General John Pershing—Commander, U.S. Army Expeditionary Force, Mexico

Vincente Conrado, Henry Parker and Pedro Quesada—Circle C cowboys

Sweet Lady Kate—Mad Mady's employee

Elodie Saint-Sauveur—War Nurse, Rouen, France

Coyote—Humorous and dangerous wild dog and cultural hero

PROLOGUE
NEW SPAIN

New Spain, a territorial region of the Spanish Empire during the colonization of the Americas, included present-day Mexico, the U.S. Southwest, California and parts of Central America. In 1521, the Spanish conquered the Aztecs and named the region˙ The Kingdom of New Spain with the capital in Mexico City on the site of the Aztec Empire.

In 1540, Spanish Conquistadors ventured from Mexico City to New Spain's northern regions. The captain general of this expedition was Francisco Vasquez de Coronado y Lujan. Coronado was a governor of a Nueva Galicia, a New Spain province. He was driven to lead an expedition by stories of Native American cities containing vast riches.

Coronado commanded some 400 Spanish soldiers who wore brimmed helmets and light body armor. They were well-armed. Some soldiers had pikes, others had muskets or crossbows. Every soldier carried a sword. Several Franciscan friars and about 1,500 Indians were also among the explorers. The expedition included herds of horses, mules, cattle and sheep.

Beyond territorial expansion of New Spain, Coronado pursued gold and glory believed to be in the Seven Cities of Cibola: Spanish for the Zuni pueblos and the surrounding regions. The legendary cities of magnificent treasures and gold were sought by sixteenth century Spanish explorers, with Coronado among the most prominent. Legend has it that the Cities of Gold are located throughout the pueblos of Arizona and New Mexico.

Coronado's northward trek followed the Gulf of California to the Spanish settlement of Culiacan, located in a valley on the slopes of the Sierra Madre Mountains. Then, the Rio Sonora was followed to its source where a mountain pass was found to present day Arizona. There on flat ground, Coronado and the expedition arrived at a village with great disappointment. Rather than encountering a fabulous city of gold, they found adobe Zuni pueblos.

The expedition continued on to the Colorado River. At that juncture, they moved east to pueblos in New Mexico. Instead, of Cities of Gold, Coronado found the Rio Grande Valley. Another disappointment. The Rio Grande flowed through vast high-desert areas providing widespread irrigation for the inhabitants. The Tiguex Province, named by the Spanish, consisted of several prosperous pueblo communities near present-day Bernalillo, New Mexico.

At first, the Tiwa pueblos Indians welcomed the drained men and provided resources. The expedition wintering in Bernalillo. Pueblo generosity ended as the Spanish prolonged their stay and continued to demand resources. A battle ensued between the pueblos of Tiwa and the Spanish. The Tiguex War was one of the first between Europeans and Native Americans.

Finally, the expedition pressed on to Kansas in the hopes of finding Quivira, a village said to be filled with gold. Instead, the plains were filled with buffalo. In the end, the explorer-soldiers covered vast areas of land and claimed territory, but no city of gold or treasures. In 1542, Coronado began the journey back to Mexico City. From his perspective, the expedition was a failure. He did not find Cities of Gold, but he is one of the first to travel to American West regions never explored by Europeans and found the Grand Canyon.

Back in Mexico, Francisco Vazquez de Coronado y Lujan Coronado returned to his position as governor of Nueva Galicia and to investigations into his leadership during the expedition. Although vindicated, he was eventually dismissed as governor.

Whether charting territories or seeking treasure, the Spanish adventurers encountered the Sandia Mountains, which magnificently capture the essence of the high desert. Over time, Spanish settlements developed along the *El Camino Real de Tierra Adentro* that connected Mexico City to Santa Fe, including Albuquerque and Valtura, New Mexico.

PART ONE

CIRCLE C RANCH

VALTURA, NEW MEXICO

CHAPTER 1

COOPER'S HAWKS

Circle C Ranch, New Mexico
March 1916

On this striking New Mexico morning, the late winter sun suspended in a cloudless blue sky seems more like a spring sun. The high-desert sage is in bloom, with its rugged beauty arrayed across the vast majestic mesa. Cooper's Hawks circle the sky and charge the vacant sunlight with chilling cries. The North American hawks are natural predators to almost all smaller birds.

New Mexico is home to many kinds of hawks with the Cooper's Hawks being the most in number throughout the state. This gray back hawk inhabits large trees and is about seventeen inches long with a wingspan of thirty inches. When hunting smaller birds, the Cooper's Hawk suddenly appears at high speed to pursue and capture its prey.

Mounted on a bay horse called Patriot is a cowboy in a white shirt and dark brown pants; he pulls down the brim of his Stetson against the sun. He is Aldoloreto "Adobe" Centori, owner and operator of the Circle C Ranch.

Between the *bosque* and the mesa stands a large herd of cattle, most of which carry a "C" inside a circle brand. Spanish for woodlands, the *bosque* follows the *Rio Grande* as a wide band of cottonwood trees and mesquite. It extends 200 miles from Socorro in the south to Cochiti Pueblo in the north.

This morning, Centori is at the vanguard of experienced cowboys who are scattered in small groups ready for work. His face, with strong features and square jaw line, shows a dark red stubble and blue eyes that survey the herd. Most women think he is handsome. The Spanish-American War veteran is friendly with all types of people without ingratiation. Once his word is given, it is not broken. He has spent most of his forty-five years developing self-reliance. It began on the sidewalks of New York that provided him with valuable lessons in resourcefulness.

Centori runs the Circle C with a keen regard for economy and a capacity for productive ranching. He is an excellent leader with a talent for motivating men. Circle C cowboys are decisively loyal to him. The Circle C Ranch is located several miles north of Valtura in Corona County and 20 miles north of Albuquerque, on almost 50,000 acres. Native Americans, Spaniards and Americans occupied this land over the centuries. Over the years, he has expanded its acreage and has become the largest rancher in Corona County.

A true New Mexican, in experience if not in lineage, Centori has a decided love of the new state's stunning landscapes, striking architecture, green chile cooking and beautiful women. He is a charismatic, somewhat inscrutable, son of New York and adopted son of New Mexico.

Circle C foreman Francisco Griegos sits on his gray horse next to Centori, looking formidable. He wears a wide flat top hat that has a chinstrap. An embroidered cotton shirt is under an open jacket. A gust of wind sends up his red silk scarf. Some years as a Mexican vaquero strengthened his stature as a New Mexico cowboy.

At first, he appears to be uncompromising, but Griegos is highly regarded at the Circle C Ranch. Whenever a cowboy is in need, he is quick to offer help, devoting himself to the issue. He is somewhat younger than Centori and is married to a beautiful woman. He is a key contributor to the operations of the Circle C. When Centori is away from the ranch—Griegos is in charge.

Circle C men, including seasoned cowboys Pedro Quesada and Vicente Conrado, and younger men like Henry Parker, are poised to ride the range and find cattle. Their job in the spring roundup is to brand new calves, or mavericks, before releasing them to the range.

"Another roundup, Francisco," Centori reflects.

"Yes, it sure is, Boss."

"Sometimes I miss the open range days. Before barbed wire, this job was exhausting mayhem, but we would meet old friends and make new ones."

"That was a little before my time."

"I know, probably been over longer than I think. It's different now with each rancher's cattle on a home range."

"The Circle C range has good grazing."

"This is a good place to raise cattle and a good place to live," Centori adds.

Griegos shifts in his saddle before saying, "I had that feeling the first time I saw this spread...and was convinced after meeting you and A.P."

"A.P. Baker was a good man and a good friend. He made people feel better when they were down. He was one of the best men I ever knew. I miss him."

"We all do, Boss. He never lied, never cheated and never apologized."

"Ha, that's true, and he offered sage advice."

"He sure did."

"One piece of advice stays with me—it is okay to look back, just don't stare too long."

"Sounds like excellent advice."

"I try to follow it."

"A.P. could drink any man under the table in good times, but he would not drink at all in bad times," Griegos recalls.

"That sounds about right...A.P. was replaced by a fine man, second to none."

"Thanks for saying so, Boss, but no one could replace A.P."

Moving away from the painful subject, Centori states, "With the price of beef close to twenty-nine cents a pound, it should be a record-breaking year for cattle ranchers."

Taking the cue, Griegos follows, "I guess that big trouble over in Europe has something to do with that price jump."

"Afraid so," Centori agrees, "but that's the market and we will serve it while we can. We are detached from the European war, but the distant battle has implications for the U.S. beyond the price of beef."

"You could be right, but I hope you are wrong. The president is campaigning for re-election on a promise to keep America out of the war," Griegos replies.

"Yes, that's what Wilson says, but U.S. Allies are gravely entangled. Armies have dug in on the Western Front—in trenches. It is an extremely deadly deal, with tanks, accurate artillery and even gas attacks. The British and French are expecting American aid from hope, if not from desperation."

"I can't picture the U.S. getting involved in that bloodbath. Besides, we are still an ocean away."

"An ocean patrolled by German submarines," Centori counters. "It is a matter of time before American supply ships are attacked, drawing us into the war."

"Hope you are wrong about that, Boss. Mexico is a much closer concern. The Mexican revolution is spilling over to our side of the border."

"The border troubles seem connected to the war in France. European involvement would make that situation much more dangerous. Anyway, I am sure the Pancho Villa raid will be answered," Centori says while looking over the mountains as if seeing the ocean beyond and hearing distant drumbeats. "Don't forget the *Lusitania* was torpedoed by a German submarine."

"Over a thousand people were killed in the sinking," Griegos adds.

"Including 128 Americans. The ship most likely carried war materiel for England from New York. The name Jennifer Prower appeared on the victims' list."

"Jennifer? You knew her in Valtura and in New York!"

"Thought I knew her. It was a treacherous ride that started in New Mexico and ended in New York. She was deadly, with a heart of stone. As the publisher of the *Valtura Journal*, she specialized in German intelligence collection and seduction. She shocked my senses. Her sorcery worked on me."

Griegos brings him back to the present, "I wondered what happened to her."

"I stopped wondering until I heard about the *Lusitania*. Ironic, a German spy killed by a German submarine...she got A.P. killed."

Griegos frowns, this time he changes the subject, "The other livestock producers in New Mexico are sure to do as well in the market."

"No doubt they are all free-market capitalists," Centori exclaims.

"Your cattle growers' association has improved the market as well."

"It is not exactly *my* association; I just try to lend a hand."

"Okay, if increasing profits and protecting ranchers' rights is just lending a hand!"

As a preeminent New Mexico rancher, Centori was a primary force behind the creation of the New Mexico Cattle Growers' Association. He works to promote the economic health of the industry.

That morning before sunrise, the first thing he realized was her absence. In the middle of the night, Mad Mady Blaylock left the Circle C and his bed. Before her frequent visits, he had kept her at arm's length—more than a woman should tolerate. More than most women *would* tolerate. Mad Mady was not most women. She played the cards that were dealt to her. That may have been a miscalculation.

After Centori's New York adventure where German agents and his own Mata Hari were defeated, he retired as Corona Country sheriff and focused on the ranch and on Mad Mady. Finally, it seemed natural for Mady to come to the Circle C ranch. Then, her increased visits seemed unnatural. Now she is gone.

Drawing a slow breath, Centori tries to dismiss this morning's surprise and any mistakes and regrets. Yet, Mady's abrupt departure left him wondering about further dialogue, if there is anything more to say. He reins to the right and reaches for a canteen, causing the saddle to creak. Urging Patriot forward, his thoughts slip back to Mady and the events that brought them together. Only gradually did he realize that those same events could tear them apart.

Above, the hawks in flight communicate with piercing calls, sounds, displays, and glide in a natural pattern. Most of the grand birds mate for life. Centori returns the canteen and wonders about the years with Mady and if they could mate for life.

In those perplexing years, their motives may have been repressed and below explanation. Mady, acting as a prosecuting attorney, would say Centori thinks of love not as a means but as an end. That indictment is at odds with his view of himself. Emotions that expressed in various combinations are not transparent. In a curious part of her charge, he walks the razor's edge between passion and love. A coyote howls in the distance. Centori turns his head.

At times, she was headstrong. At other times, she retreated from histrionics to examine their issues. This significant part of their dialogue allowed her to ask important questions. She seldom liked the answers. Overall, he is honorable in relating to Mady. At least that is how he understands himself.

A sharp cry in the sky breaks Centori's concentration. He looks upward where hawks appear to float in a sweeping pattern. Female hawks seek a mate by sending reassuring calls. He wonders if Mady is right about a darker reason for their problems, darker than he is willing to admit. Although falsely committed, Mady spent time in the Territorial Insane Asylum; she sometimes thought he was a more worthy patient.

Centori takes off the Stetson, pushes his hair back and replaces the cowboy hat. While he does this, two hawks engage in a mating flight, distracting his meditation. With wings high above, the male hawk dives toward the female and slowly flies around, rhythmically flapping. After agreement, the pair will make a nest. Centori and Patriot move forward in a stately lope. Patriot produces a smart snort in reaction to the birds.

Returning to his thoughts, Centori does not expect the same elation for Mady as he had for Gabriela Zena—most people are better in the abstract. Gabriela, a beautiful Cuban nationalist, loved him within the context of politics. She ignored political differences during intimate times. The Spanish-American War had brought them together; the legacy of the Mexican-American war treaty had forced them apart.

Mady never tried to compete with her. Instead, she used empathy in the hope of exorcising the ghost, imploring him not to settle for a memory. He is unable to drive the spirit from his mind. Nevertheless, Gabriela's ghost is no barrier to loving other women. The hawks return to chilling cries as to punctuate the problem. Centori takes a deep breath, exhales and sees the hawks moving through the trees.

German secret agent Jennifer Prower handed further frustration to Mady's pursuit of Centori. He was attracted to this desirable and dangerous woman—to his detriment. Unlike Gabriela, Jennifer never loved him and probably hated him. Beauty disguises many dangers. In the end, Centori learned that she was a German spy. If every man must play the fool once in a lifetime, Centori did so with Jennifer Prower.

CHAPTER 2

FLASH OF LIGHTNING

Although the warm day is uncomfortable for the cowboys, the more than 2,000 white-faced Herefords show no indication. On the wind, the men hear the cattle's soft sound in the distance drifting through the air.

Cattle is as much a part of the New Mexico landscape as the national environment. Spanish cattle arrived in Mexico with Hernan Cortes in the 16th century. Those longhorns eventually moved north and became plentiful in the Americas. Cattle ultimately replaced the decimated bison despite the fact that bison are more adaptable to arid environments. Over the centuries, cattle ranches became plentiful in Mexico, Texas and New Mexico.

Centori turns Patriot's head for the *bosque*; he hears a distant rumble and stops. Griegos hears it too. A glance passes between the two cowboys acknowledging the muffled sounds of horses on the move. Hoof beats pounding the ground are becoming closer and louder. Two silhouettes on the horizon, men on horseback, spur forward from the south.

From the dust, two spectral figures, dressed in army khaki and campaign hats, are approaching. Intrigue flashes through the cowboys at the sight of soldiers coming into focus, completing the surprise. Their eyes register the fast approaching cavalrymen moving with the grace of lifelong riders. They are not slow in detecting the importance of the visitors. The next seconds seem interminable. The soldiers pull up and the lead horse jerks its head and neighs.

"Mr. Centori?" shouts one of the mounted soldiers.

Making eye contact, "I am Adobe Centori. How can I help you, Captain?"

"I'm Captain Aragon and this is Sergeant Barela. General Pershing sent us."

"Is that right?"

"Yes, sir."

"What brings you here on his behalf?" Centori turns in his saddle toward Griegos.

"The general wishes to see you and he invites you to Camp Furlong."

Captain Aragon, with dark hair close to his collar, looks at Centori who pulls up the brim of his hat. With piercing eyes he studies the soldiers and asks, "They sent you all the way from Camp Furlong to find me?"

"We were already in Albuquerque," Aragon replies.

"What's this all about, Captain?"

Aragon reaches under his tunic for an envelope, holds it high and asserts, "Here's a sealed message from General Pershing."

Centori stares at Aragon before accepting and pocketing the envelope, "When does the general expect me?"

The captain replies, "Mr. Centori, my orders are to deliver the message, nothing more. I believe the general would have provided details in the letter."

"Okay, Captain Aragon. You are riding a fine horse. What's his name?"

"Relampajo!"

"Flash of Lightning," Griegos says.

"Yes. He is that fast!"

"He could probably be a great racing horse. Tell General Pershing I will see him as soon as I can," Centori offers.

"Thank you, I will do so. Good day to you gentlemen," Aragon states.

The soldiers turn their horses and thunder off leaving a cloud of dust in their wake.

Centori senses what Griegos is thinking and says, "This note is too serious not to command concern."

As the riders fade, Griegos exclaims, "I'm concerned about the roundup!"

"This could be good for business and supplying beef to the army is patriotic. We both know you can handle things just fine."

The two cowboys view the departing soldiers who are urging their horses onward. When the silence becomes too heavy, Griegos exclaims, "*Mi Dios*, you don't even know what's in the note!"

Listening to a coyote cry, Centori's lips tighten before he responds, "I think I do."

Griegos smiles and appears amused by the concise comment. Reaching the horizon, the riders let their horses out and gallop out of sight.

Conrado and Quesada ride up to Centori and Griegos. Quesada asks, "*Quiénes son esos hombres, jefe?*

"*Soldados con un mensaje de un viejo soldado,*" Centori replies.

The cowboys speak no more of the visitors. They return to the matter at hand, and spread out to search for Circle C cattle. In the distance, a band of coyotes accompanies the lone coyote howl. They chime in, as if on cue.

***

After a long day in the saddle, the cowboys find relief as the warm day yields to a cool twilight. Day one of the roundup achieved some of the expected results, but it was not an auspicious start. After they branded scores of mavericks, a late afternoon rainstorm with loud thunder scattered the herd and reduced visibility. The roundup was somewhat slowed. It will take a few more days to find most of the calves. It could take longer for Centori to come to terms with Pershing's message.

CHAPTER 3

SANCTUM SANCTORUM

It is a typical March day with bright sun and a mild breeze as the cowboys ride the range to gather the rest of roaming calves for spring branding. Centori is uneasy about General Pershing's request. The demands of the roundup do little to assuage those feelings. He silently reflects on his indecisiveness.

As usual, the late afternoon sun settles in the west turning the Sandia Mountains a bright watermelon red, signaling an end to the day. They will continue in the morning with or without Centori.

With the day's work done they head back to the ranch house. Centori, Griegos and their cowboys enjoy a dinner of chicken, beans and green chile peppers. Later that evening, Centori sits with Pershing's note on the front porch in the last light of the day. The vigas, round logs used as posts and overhead beams, appear especially vivid at this time.

As the sun sets behind the Circle C Ranch house, he goes into the library for a Jameson Irish whiskey and a Cuban cigar, Romeo and Juliette. He burns some dried sage. Burning the dried flowering plant provides a purifying aroma. Used in smudging rituals, burning sage gives a spiritual cleansing, replacing negative energy with positive energy. Then, he pours a drink and lights his cigar.

This secluded, and at times enigmatic, part of the house is his *sanctum sanctorum*. The library provides tranquil time the moment he enters. Occasionally, that silence is disturbed. This is true tonight. Ghosts seem to occupy the room, or just one. Although Gabriela never set foot in the Circle C, he senses her essence. He tries to be vigilant against her consuming too much time, with some success.

To this day, Centori never regretted and never forgot this star-crossed affair. Heartbreak settled into his soul and remains a permanent part of his existence. He had loved Gabriela as much as a man can love a woman and he could not stop loving her in his mind. The romance ended in despair; she remains as no mere memory. Real or perceived, she was and always will be the love of his life. When he contemplates their good days, he remembers what they thought. In his heart, they are alone together. It always will be so—always lovers. True love to that degree has an enduring impact that never ends, providing that true love exists at all.

"The Lord is near to the broken hearted and saves the crushed in spirit," wrote King David in a psalm. Adobe Centori received no such salvation. Gabriela died in Chaco Canyon. It was autumn. She was 33. Inwardly he feels responsible for her death; yet outwardly, he insists that he is all right. He is not, as Mady or any other woman would come to realize.

The large library contains a smell of leather and wood and opens onto a small *placita*. Rough-cut bookcases containing many books cover one wall. Indian art covers the other walls. On the wall behind his desk is an old photograph of his parents. His family was among the first wave of Italian immigrants to arrive in America. Having fine representation of a distinguished Roman ancestry, his heritage influences his strong bearing.

Next to that photograph is a framed letter acknowledging his statehood involvement. He was an intrepid supporter of New Mexico statehood. Intriguing experiences as a Corona County statehood and constitutional delegate contributed to his political acumen. Partisan politics in Santa Fe and in Washington had prevented statehood. New Mexico's large foreign population, taxes, and the role of the Catholic Church were points of contention. Finally, the tumult ended with New Mexico achieving statehood in 1912.

Beyond his contributions to statehood, Centori covertly prevented a war with Mexico without letters, accolades or awards. Emerging from the internal conflicts in Santa Fe, he became a prominent citizen of the new 47th state. Whether riding up San Juan Hill in Cuba or riding the range in New Mexico, Centori expresses indomitable will and confident leadership ability.

The serenity of the library will be short-lived. Having absorbed the impact of Pershing's words, Centori attempts to decipher the meaning.

Ironically, he listens to Puccini's *La Fanciulla del West* (*The Girl of the West*). The opera, which premiered at the New York Metropolitan Opera in 1910, features a saloon owner named Minnie. As the soprano blares from the Victrola, he closes his eyes and thinks of another saloon owner, but not for long. He sips the whiskey and reads the note again, as if something new would appear. Without complete information, he regrets accepting the meeting.

The Victrola suddenly stops; the music is gone. Thoughts of Mad Mady are gone. He has no instinct to ride to Mad Mady's Saloon in Valtura. Instead, he takes a slow draw on his cigar, adjusts the music player and returns to the note. *Pershing wants to discuss a proposal, but the note provides no details. The army may need a beef supplier, but why not say so. How can I make such a long trip without knowing the details? I already gave my word to Captain Aragon.*

Centori steps outside, faces the shadows of the fading light and stoically smokes his cigar. There are no answers outside. He returns to the library. Draining the whiskey glass, he stands and stares into the cold fireplace. *The proposal must be confidential, and he could not provide specific information.*

Taking another slow puff from the Romeo and Juliette, he re-reads the last sentence and stares at the books that fill the shelves apparently searching the titles that may provide answers. He jumps up, paces the wood floor of the library and thinks about war and the prospect of repeating the experience. After returning from Cuba, he knows he is different but conceals any change.

Opening a large, weather-beaten wooden door, he steps outside and scans the night sky. A vast blanket of stars seems shrouded in darkness, despite the moonlight. Looking at the distant flickering lights of Valtura, he wonders which light is Mad Mady's Saloon. The wind carries the slight moan of a woman in distress, real or imagined. Whichever the case, he has stopped fearing the banshee.

Beyond the mystery, the request from a prominent general is flattering, but this does nothing to ease his concern. The issue remains unresolved; Centori remains unsettled. *La Fanciulla del West* ends. He digs out a photo of Gabriela as if she will play a significant role in his choice.

***

The morning sun, about to rise over the Sandia Mountains, will gently send light into this part of the world. Centori stands on the porch with a proper cup of strong black coffee and consider his night of fitful sleep.

The significance of Pershing's note filled his night, and now fills another day at the Circle C Ranch. Centori blankly waves at Greigos who walks to the horse barn with a ching sound of spurs in his steps. At the nearby corral, Centori sees Pedro Quesada and Vicente Conrado rest their arms on the fence rail and watch Henry Parker exercise a horse.

Centori faces a bright morning and a long train ride to Camp Furlong. Gabriela, who returned to his dreams, may have cast the deciding vote in favor of meeting Pershing.

CHAPTER 4

COYOTE CRY

Uncomfortable in a first class railcar of the Atchison, Topeka and Santa Fe, Centori travels to Camp Furlong with mixed feelings. In 1912, the army post formed in Luna County because of the growing border tensions. He continues to turn over the note in his mind, *The border trouble and the Columbus raid probably prompted this...but what exactly does the general want of me?*

Pershing was with the 10th Cavalry Regiment as a first lieutenant in the Spanish-American War. At the battle of San Juan Hill, Centori and Pershing were recognized for gallantry. The rails continue to sound the progress south to El Paso, Texas. *Is he offering a position? What kind? Hmm...the kind that is too confidential to reduce to writing.*

Centori is well aware of the Mexican revolution, the placement of U.S. troops on the border—and the secret Revert Document that endangered New Mexico statehood. His knowledge of the U.S. violation of the Treaty of Mesilla and his involvement with the Revert Document remain factors in political issues.

It can't be about the dead and buried Revert Document. How many know the U.S. violated a treaty and that New Mexico and Arizona had actually reverted to Mexico days before statehood? No, I would have heard from John Murphy but not a word about the border tensions that preceded the Columbus attack.

When President Woodrow Wilson condemned Mexico's revolutionary government, attacks on Americans and American property increased. Mexican bandits robbed an American train north of the border, killing three Americans. This assured escalation as Wilson sent more soldiers to defend the border at Brownsville, Texas, and at Douglas, Arizona. Then, Wilson recognized Venustiano Carranza, an enemy of revolutionary leader Francisco "Pancho" Villa, as Mexican president. This action contributed to the growing unrest and to Villa's unrest. In addition, U.S. Signal Corps planes monitoring Villa's army on the border encountered machine gun attacks, but safely returned to Fort Brown in Brownsville, Texas.

When Villa's army attacked Columbus, Southern Department commander General Frederick Funston recommended a direct pursuit in Mexico. Wilson agreed and issued orders to Pershing to command an invading army to capture Villa and prevent further attacks on America.

"EL PASO, next stop El Paso," cries the train conductor as the rhythm of the rails slows down.

Once inside the Union Depot, some 300 miles from Valtura, Centori notices the large windows streaming sunlight in the central room illuminating a newsstand. Newspapers across the country ran stories about Pancho Villa's raid on Columbus, New Mexico that killed 16 civilians and 37 soldiers; the *El Paso Herald* is no exception.

Villa and 500 mounted men charged into Columbus, the small border town near the 13th U.S. Calvary garrison at Camp Furlong. The raiders burned buildings and damaged the town. They had many casualties before 300 cavalry troopers forced a retreat. Villa's invasion of Columbus caused public outcry.

New Mexican National Guard units came into federal service to defend the border in San Antonio, El Paso, Nogales and Brownsville.

The U.S. Army increased border patrols and the president ordered an army under General Pershing into Mexico to capture or kill Villa. Pershing, commander at Camp Furlong, is receiving men and supplies. Regiments of infantry and cavalry, and a Signal Corps company are preparing for the Mexican Punitive Expedition. Armored motor vehicles, field artilleries, aero squadrons, engineers and ambulance companies are assembling at the camp.

Centori folds his newspaper, places it under his arm and boards a train of the Southern Pacific Railroad to Deming, New Mexico. This large town in Luna County is 33 miles from the Mexican border. Before the Gadsden Purchase, the town was on the Mexican border.

***

Having traveled the rails for an additional 80 miles, Centori arrives in Deming, the county seat. That is the point where the AT&SF joined the Southern Pacific Railway, creating the second transcontinental railroad. A final silver spike, connecting the U.S. from ocean to ocean for a second time, celebrated the 1881 event.

Standing in front of the large two-story station, Centori waits alone. A coyote cry springs from nowhere. He looks around the flat land that spreads to the horizon in all directions—and sees no living thing.

CHAPTER 5

CAMP FURLONG

General Pershing's note said an officer in an army staff motorcar would be waiting to provide transportation to the camp. Coyote cries ring out, perhaps heralding Centori's arrival or the approaching motorcar that rumbles to a stop, silencing the coyotes.

"Mr. Centori!" shouts a young officer from the window. On the double, he opens the back door and announces, "I'm Lieutenant Pargas here to transport you to Camp Furlong. Sorry I'm late."

"You are not late, Lieutenant, and thanks!"

Centori tosses his bag inside and sits in the back seat.

"How was your trip, Mr. Centori?"

"Tolerable."

"Have you ever been to Camp Furlong?"

"No, I have not. I expect an impressive facility, since it's the headquarters for the 13th Cavalry."

"That's right. The camp expanded rapidly after the Columbus raid. We have about 5,000 men, including New Mexico National Guard units, and the 1st Aero Squadron. We will not be surprised by General Villa again, at least not in Columbus."

"General Villa!"

"Anyone who gathers 500 men is called general," Pargas retorts.

Centori smiles and says, "Aero Squadron? That is very interesting."

"We are ready. Protection and preparation___" Pargas stops short and falls silent.

During the remainder of the ride, Centori mentally rehearses what he will say to the general, given various possibilities. At Camp Furlong, they ride through an array of hundreds of tents and wooden buildings including barracks, supply depots and motor repair facilities. The post is lively with solders in khaki uniforms and campaign hats. Stopping at the HQ building, Pargas escorts Centori to the office of General John "Black Jack" Pershing.

"This is the general's office, Mr. Centori," Pargas says before jumping out and knocking on the door.

"Thanks again, Lieutenant, and good luck."

"Good luck to you too, Mr. Centori."

Behind the opened door is Master Sergeant Alarid who ushers the guest inside.

General Pershing stands and emerges from behind his desk the moment Centori enters and offers his hand, "Welcome to Camp Furlong, Mr. Centori."

"General," he shows little emotion, resisting an instinct to salute.

Pershing is not alone. His retinue includes top staff officers who have top-secret security clearances. Centori quickly studies the men around the room, inhales slightly and removes his Stetson.

After introducing the officers, including Camp Commander Colonel H.J. Slocum, Pershing says, "Have a seat." It almost sounded like an order.

Centori settles into a chair, his eyes surveying the office. The general sits down and moves a stack of papers before offering, "Thank you for coming. I know it is not an easy journey. Would you like a drink, Mr. Centori? Or should I call you captain?"

Somewhat puzzled he replies, "General, I'm not a day drinker and it has been a long time since I held that rank."

Pershing pushes files on the desk aside and says, "So, you have quite a cattle ranch near Albuquerque."

"Closer to Valtura, in Corona County, just north of Bernalillo County," he replies while adjusting to the interior light.

"I understand you are a leader with the New Mexico Cattle Growers' Association as well."

"Yes, General, you could say that, but I don't think you invited me to discuss my business," he says with a slight smile while hoping not to offend.

"No, I did not. You must be eager to learn the reason for the meeting. I will get to the point. I am sure you heard about the unfortunate business in Columbus."

"Villa. It is front-page news across the country. Cavalry engaged him in the town."

"That's right. Our 13th Cavalry, with about two hundred and forty men, repelled Villa's army of about five hundred men. We resisted and beat them back to Mexico."

"I read about the fight; I'm not surprised by the result."

"Spoken like an old cavalry officer."

"Not so old," Centori quips, feeling more comfortable in the room.

"We did have casualties," Pershing laments, "and the invaders burned buildings and killed civilians. The action of the machine gunners was decisive in driving Villa's army out. Lieutenant John Lucas of the 13th Cavalry commanded the machine gun troop."

"General Pershing, you may remember me from Cuba. We met briefly after San Juan Hill."

"You were valiant in Cuba," he says showing little recollection of meeting him.

"That depends on which stories you hear."

Pershing reaches into an open drawer and places a file on the desk, "Your military record is impressive."

"I see," Centori offers with a blank face.

"This file states that you were highly decorated for action in Cuba. You returned from the war with a reputation for daring, quick action and enduring courage."

"Many men did more."

"Courageous and modest," Pershing adds.

"Why am I here, General?"

"And straightforward too."

"Your note is vague. I understand that, but imagine my curiosity. What can I do for you, Sir?"

Pershing smiles before continuing his narrative, "We should get down to business. Villa's attack on Columbus must be answered."

"Beyond beating him back to Mexico?"

Pershing stands, glances at his staff, moves to the window and looks south, "We are organizing a punitive expedition into Mexico."

"Yes, I read about that possibility," Centori underestimates his interest.

Pershing turns back to him and replies, "It is more than a possibility. President Wilson has ordered me to lead an army into Mexico to find and capture Villa."

Centori stares back, "That is a tall order."

"Without a doubt, but the U.S. Army will be up to the job. I am pulling together a force of three brigades. We will take the field with four cavalry regiments and two infantry regiments; attached will be the 6th Field Artillery, along with engineers and other supporting units."

"Well, general, that sounds like a formidable force, but why are you telling me, a civilian, all this?"

"I am telling this to a highly decorated army officer."

"Ex-army officer."

"You are a combat veteran. Your record speaks for itself."

"All the same, what does it have to do with me?" Centori questions while having a good idea of the answer.

"When we cross the border into Mexico, we will be followed by the 5th Cavalry and two more infantry regiments," Pershing reveals his plan and waits. Centori provides no visible reaction as the general returns to his chair and continues, "We are recruiting officers for key positions. We are recruiting experienced, resourceful men with sharp leadership skills."

Colonel Slocum nods in agreement while looking at Centori, who waits for the inevitable.

"Mr. Centori, I would like you to command the 5th Cavalry! I am prepared to offer you a commission as a full colonel to lead the regiment." He pauses for effect. "With your military record and familiarity of this terrain, I know you will be successful with this commission."

Centori absorbs the significant statement and thinks about a response. The others study him for a reaction.

Pershing adds, "Your cavalrymen will be armed with Springfield rifles and semi-automatic pistols."

"General, that is quite a vote of confidence...thank you."

"Then you accept?"

"Taking all circumstances into account, I don't think I'm the man for the job. Much has changed since I last served."

His negative response changes the faces around the room. Pershing waits for the uncomfortable quiet to register. Then, with a thin smile, he stands without looking down from 'on high' and asks, "Are you sure?"

Centori's sense of adventure causes him to hesitate, providing Pershing with an opening, "What if I said your friend John Murphy was offered a commission in the 6th Cavalry Regiment?"

"Murphy?"

"That's right. You are here on your record and on Murphy's recommendation."

Centori's shoulders slump; he wonders if Pershing knows the highly classified information surrounding the Revert Document. He straightened his back, his face becomes stony, "General, I have served this country since my youth. In that time, I have helped to bring triumph to America's fights. Openly, on the battlefields of Cuba and___"

"No need to pause. Issues relating to a certain document and action against German saboteurs in your file are classified and will remain secret."

Centori's eyes widen as he realizes the extent of Pershing briefing. Reacting to the revelation he asks, "Is there anything you don't know?"

Closing the short space separating them, Pershing stares, "I don't know if your answer is final."

Centori studies the cover of his closed file, somewhat lost for words.

"Yet, I do know that the expedition can use your leadership."

Pondering the statement, he slowly shakes his head and replies, "You have overestimated me. I am a cattleman about to start the spring roundup. Time is an issue for me. I came out of respect for you, General."

"That is not lost on me, Mr. Centori."

"I can't rejoin the army for an unknown period of time."

"Are you sure?"

"Plenty sure, General."

"Perhaps you will think again. You would be well-advised to at least reconsider."

Pershing's words sound like a challenge, or a dare. Will the great Centori rise to the challenge and live up to his reputation? His fascination peaks before saying, "That could take time."

"Time is one thing we have little of," Pershing declares.

"I can't make a decision on the spot," he equivocates. "I will give the situation more thought."

"Thank you. You have given much to your country. I will respect your decision."

"I appreciate that, General. I will answer within 48 hours."

"Now, you may miss army cooking, so please join me in the officers' mess hall. After the meal, you will be more enthusiastic about re-joining this man's army."

With a wide smile, Centori reacts with crisp confidence, "Army cooking will not help, General!"

CHAPTER 6

HOLD YOUR HORSES

On the train back to Valtura, Centori weighs the prospect of an ambitious adventure, with calculated risk. The rhythm of the rails seems to sound like *got-to-decide, got-to decide, got-to-decide.* Pershing skillfully applied pressure in a room filled with high-ranking military officers. Centori rejects directives of other men. He makes exceptions for the military and its chain of command, but he is a civilian. Even so, Pershing appealed to an American patriot's willingness to serve. All considered he remains indecisive about answering the latest call of duty.

***

Now, on a warm morning, Centori enters the Circle C horse barn, moves along the row of horses and checks the stalls. Although consumed with ranch business and the roundup, the thought of Camp Furlong remains distracting. He has thought of little else since the meeting. On the walk through, he notes the water buckets, hay nets and the well-being of the horses.

Reaching Patriot's stall, he sees the bay horse is restless and needs exercise. He talks to the jumpy stallion and moves outside to the approaching Griegos.

"Good morning, Boss."

"Seems like I have been away for a while."

"The boys are doing well with the roundup."

"I am sure of that."

"What was so important about the general's meeting?"

"He gave me much to think about."

"Does he want you to be a general?" Griegos jokes.

"Close—a colonel."

Griegos' smile disappears, "This has to do with Villa."

"Yes, the expedition into Mexico to chase him down."

"Did you refuse?"

"Not exactly."

"What?"

"Francisco, I told the general he would have my answer in 48 hours. He agreed to wait."

"For what? Your decision should be easy. Your place is here at the Circle C. As a war veteran haven't you done enough for this country?"

Centori has done more than enough for his country. More than his Spanish-American War service. More than Griegos knows. His role in New Mexico statehood is unknown to Griegos given its top-secret status. He changed history for his leadership in the Revert Document crisis—with great personal sacrifice. He was not part of that story; he was the heart of that story. Yet, the top-secret nature of his heroism in saving the border territories and preventing a war with Mexico remains untold, a story that changed his life and led to regret, anger and pain. Griegos knows about Gabriela and how she pierced his heart, but little else about the Revert Document Affair.

Nor does Griegos know about his bravery in preventing a major terrorist attack in New York. He faced the challenge of German saboteurs and won. Overall, Adobe Centori performed huge acts of human and political importance.

"I have no doubt that you can run this ranch, Francisco, if I accept, but I do have doubt about the expedition."

"Thanks for your confidence. I am not certain the expedition is a wise move. Besides, the general will find someone else."

"On one hand, I feel a sense of responsibility, but there is not vast public support for pursuing Villa and he is not the legitimate leader of Mexico."

"Invading Mexico could turn an ally into an enemy," Griegos says.

"That's right," Centori agrees. "U.S. isolationism apart, the war in Europe is looming and we could be involved. Actions which can lead to a potential war with Mexico are unwise."

"Yes. Has the general considered other means of untangling border issues and securing the U.S. against further raids?"

"No. His orders are clear."

"Seems like you have made a decision."

"Not yet."

"Why not?"

"I don't know."

Achieving New Mexico statehood provided valuable foreign policy lessons for Centori. After the U.S. violated the Treaty of Mesilla, Article X, he views political issues through a lens called the Revert Document.

During the private meal in the officers' club, Pershing confided in Centori regarding political and military concerns that are at odds. Washington placed restrictions on the mission, calling its success into question. Pershing expressed a lack of confidence in local support in Mexico—and anticipated hostility.

He said the expedition would be without the support of Mexican President Venustiano Carranza who thinks of it as an invasion. Although honest about the mission, Pershing was not a great salesman.

"Oh, I almost forgot," Griegos says, "You received this note while you were gone. It's from Justo Calabaza."

"Another note!" Centori exclaims.

"Hold your horses; he is not a general."

PART TWO

LOST CITY OF CIBOLA

CHAPTER 7

MAD MADY'S SALOON

In the midst of the chatter and the smell of beer and tobacco, Adobe Centori sits at the bar of Mad Mady's Saloon. The four men to his right are drinking beer and having a lively talk about Pancho Villa. The two men to his left are downing whiskey and discussing, with equal animation, the prospect of the Mexican Expedition. Other men are exchanging opinions on the war in Europe—and the possible involvement of the United States.

While Centori sips a Jameson, he listens to different points of view on international affairs, especially the debate about General Pershing's expedition. His mind goes in different directions. The general is waiting for his answer and he has not made a final decision. Now, he will meet Justo Calabaza and face another decision.

The large bar room has tables and chairs throughout the floor space with small groups of people at each table. Mad Mady is not holding court at her usual corner table, now set under a French chandelier, compliments of her sister.

Mad Mady, born Elizabeth Mady Blaylock, is around forty years of age. Born in New York City, she is an attractive woman at five feet, five inches. She typically wears blue pants and a vest with a red shirt. Under her flat round hat is her wavy black hair. Mad Mady's Saloon was in business before Centori arrived in Valtura. The two former New Yorkers became friends with romantic tension.

As one of Valtura's leading citizens, most people seek to be in Mady's company. Her saloon offers whiskey, cigars, gambling and more. The upstairs of the saloon is home to perfumed, painted women.

During the Revert Document conspiracy, Mady's sister, Sharon Blaylock, a.k.a. Santa Fe Sharon, had Mady committed to the New Mexico Territorial Insane Asylum. During Mady's time as an inmate, Sharon forcibly took over the saloon and redecorated it with a French motif.

Sharon's criminal behavior resulted in her arrest and conviction on an array of felonies, including arson and acting as an accessory to murder. In the dead of winter, she escaped from a long prison sentence. However, she did not escape a raging river near the penitentiary, or so reads the official record. Sharon was presumed dead and buried in a watery grave; Mady nor anyone else mourned. The saloon slowly reverted to its original form with vestiges of French influence including the expensive chandelier above Mady's table. Keeping some of her sister's imprint was a change that Mady accepted. The "upstairs women" have not changed and still carry small claim to respectability in selling their charms.

Centori drains his glass and looks over to the entrance and then to Mady's table. It came to his attention that she fumed for a few days after abruptly disappearing from the Circle C. He hopes she has calmed down, but for now, that is another matter. Presently, he waits for an important Pueblo Indian leader. They could have arranged the meeting in the Union Hotel or anywhere else. Instead, he chose Mady's place.

After having another drink, Centori sees a stranger enter the saloon, look around and walk to a corner table. They arrive at that table at the same time. The stranger asks, "You are Adobe Centori of the Circle C Ranch?"

"I am."

"I am Justo Calabaza."

They both sit down. Calabaza begins, "Thank you for meeting me."

Centori looks across the table and shows a polite degree of interest. Calabaza with composure and passion for this meeting says, "I understand you were in Cuba."

"Yes," he replies in an inquisitive way.

"I was with the 2nd U.S. Cavalry Regiment there and before that I was an army scout. When the war started, the 2nd Cavalry was in Kansas, Colorado and New Mexico. The regiment came together in Georgia before sailing to Havana from Mobile."

"I sailed from Tampa Bay. So, we were both at San Juan Hill with General Rufus Shafer and Colonel Roosevelt."

"That's right."

Veterans have a way of accelerating trust. Both men begin to relax as Centori says, "And you are from San Marcos Pueblo." It was a statement not a question.

"Yes and no."

One of Mady's "downstairs women" races over to take orders, "What can I get you gents?"

"Another Jameson."

"Beer."

"Sure thing," she says with a smile.

"Yes *and* no." Centori repeats.

"Allow me to explain."

"Please do."

Calabaza speaks with quiet precision, "San Marcos was a large pueblo six or seven generations ago, but the revolt destroyed the pueblo. Then it was abandoned. The people became part of the Keres pueblos of Santo Domingo and Cochiti. Yet, it is our ancestral home with spiritual connections. San Marco has not been deserted; the pueblo people and the adobe structures are just separated."

"That is a nice sentiment, but you must have another reason for our meeting," Centori says with an edge of eagerness.

"A most important reason," Calabaza replies. "I wish to talk about your land."

"My land? What is there to talk about?"

"Much."

Experience has sharpened Centori's survival skills; taking a defensive posture, he gestures for Calabaza to continue.

"A large amount of your northern land is located on the Galisteo Basin, east of the Sandia Mountains and south of Santa Fe."

"That's right," Centori confirms.

"It was the land of San Marcos and of San Cristobal and Galisteo, the lost pueblos—for centuries."

Centori stares as though accused of something. Calabaza goes on, "San Marcos had significant involvement with Spanish colonizers, or conquerors, when they came north in search of gold and silver. Instead, they found pueblos and tried to convert Indians, even to the point of Spanish Jesuits building missions."

There are many pueblos in New Mexico, including Cochiti, Jemez, Sandia, Santa Ana and Santa Domingo. They are self-governed sovereign nations with their own traditions and culture.

"Yes, and the pueblo peoples came together to resist and defend their culture and religious practices from Spanish colonizers," Centori reacts, "My land was acquired in an appropriate manner."

"Of course, Mr. Centori. You would be successful against any legal claim on the Circle C, but that is not the issue."

Centori's interest peaks, "Legal claims?"

"I do not question your ownership; no one questions your ownership." He smiles with irony and continues unabated, "Before the Spanish, the pueblo was a proud and vibrant settlement with 2,000 rooms, many plazas and 600 people. We were known as Ya'atze in the Keres language."

"I understand your resentment. We both fought against the Spanish in Cuba. I believe your village became the San Marcos Pueblo Grant by an act of the Spanish king."

"You are well-informed, Mr. Centori."

"New Mexico has a rich and interesting history."

"Rich in more ways than one," Calabaza proclaims.

"What do you mean?"

"Santo Domingo and Cochiti Pueblo Indians worked the turquoise mines for centuries in the Cerrillos Hills, and after that gathered it from old mines."

"Yes, the Turquoise Trail."

"Turquoise stones were mined for use and for trade with others in the Rio Grande Valley and with the Aztecs."

Calabaza scans the saloon with concern then asks, "How long have you owned the land you call Circle C?"

The question tightens the muscles in Centori's back, "More than 10 years. What are you driving at?" Centori demands.

"I am not sure if you believe in destiny." A cowboy walks by their table. Calabaza stops for a second and waits before continuing, "I know you are an honorable man with a reputation that you deserve."

"Thank you, but what is your point? What's this all about?" Centori reacts.

He will have to wait for the answer to his question. As Mad Mady descends from the second floor and sees his distinctive hat, her smile vanishes. Passing Slim the piano player, who is banging out a tune, she barks, "Play it louder!"

CHAPTER 8

TIFFANY TURQUOISE

"What the hell!" Mad Mady thunders as she emerges from the noise and music and approaches their table. She looks at one man indifferently and grimaces at the other. Centori ventures with a frown, "Nice to see you too, Mady."

Carelessly clothed in a red shirt and blue pants, she replies, "Are you sure?"

"Yes, but I'm not sure why you left the Circle C abruptly."

"The hell you don't!" Mady yells.

"Mady, no need to shout. I'm not deaf."

"Sometimes I doubt that."

"That's not helping this situation."

"I wasn't aiming to help."

Calabaza stands and heads for the bar. Mady looks at him with little attention.

"This is hardly the time," Centori says attempting not to pursue.

"You haven't changed!"

Hard-pressed to answer, he tries, "Nobody ever does."

"How could you change *your* character? Do you even want to? It took you days to come here!"

"I was away on business..."

She cuts him off, "You had not even a hint of concern for me or my feelings!"

In view of her anguish, he softens and innocently asks, "Mady, what on earth caused you to run out in the middle of the night after more than a year?"

"When the time is right, why wait? Stop acting as if you are the injured party," Mady exclaims. She continues, "You are not that convincing!"

"Stop!" He rubs his temples, "You are killing me."

"What? You are already dead, killed by a broken-heart sickness."

"Mady, you are ruining my good humor."

"And you don't allow your humor to be bothered!" Mady declares.

He avoids eye contact and retorts, "Not if I can help it." He had heard all of her arguments, "Look, Mady, can we talk later?" he adds not seeking an encore.

About to explode, she yells, "Why? You never cared to know my feelings. Being detached is natural for you. It happens without deliberation!"

The loud music continues to provide privacy for Mady's outburst. "Come off your high horse, Adobe, it is not becoming!"

"I'd rather not discuss it now, Mady."

"You would *rather* make love to a spirit than to flesh!" She could not have made a more inflammatory remark. His face darkens. They freeze within a heavy silence. She manages to say, "Sorry for the intrusion."

"Mady, I would not choose to hurt you for anything."

"But you have hurt me," she whirls to storm through the bustling barroom; Slim bangs out an unrecognizable tune.

Mady's complaint is a plea for meaning. Centori reacts by shifting in his chair to view her retreat, feeling her resentment. She turns back with a face of stone, causing her to crash into a downstairs woman carrying a tray of drinks. The loud music muffles most of the clanging as the tray and its contents hit the floor. Calabaza, watching Mady storm off, returns to the table and comments, "I don't think she is well."

"Oh, she is well enough, perhaps too well," Centori fakes a laugh, downs the whiskey and says, "It's a long story."

"Will she calm down?"

"Nothing that a drink can't cure."

"She is very willful," Calabaza says.

"Yes, some firebrand. We have a long history together."

"It is not my business, but the way out of a desert is to ride right through."

"Sounds like good advice."

"Did you notice her jewels?"

"No, I was protecting my flanks," Centori answers.

"It was Navajo turquoise."

Navajo turquoise. Mady never decorated her body before, he thinks.

"Her jewelry brings me back to my point."

"That's good. I want to hear more."

"Native people mined and collected rich turquoise deposits in Cerrillos Hills centuries before the Spanish and Columbus too. In the Cerrillos Mining District, thousands of tons of rock were taken from Mt. Chalchihuitl. At the turn of the century, turquoise was more valuable than gold! That's when the Americans became interested."

"Yes, railroads expanded the turquoise market and fashion made it an expensive gemstone. Mining was very profitable, I appreciate the history and I would like to hear more, but not now."

"Allow me to continue. It is well known that you are a New Yorker."

"Once upon a time," Centori says with growing impatience.

"Then you may remember the American Turquoise Company."

Mady returns with fresh drinks, "Here is another round of drinks."

Despite Mady's purposeful, casual tone, they sense the tension under her words. She then fades into the crowd, still a little embarrassed about her outburst.

"Mr. Centori, the famous New York jeweler Tiffany was behind the American Turquoise Company. Tiffany purchased the most promising mines on Turquoise Hill in Cerrillos. It was a first-rate deal for the jeweler. Tiffany turquoise mines yielded a quarter of a million dollars a year during the best years."

Centori half listens as the explanation continues and then says, "Mr. Calabaza, I'm sure you have an important point somewhere."

Reacting to the sharp statement, Calabaza falls deeper into his chair.

"Sorry. It was a mistake to meet here. I am familiar with Tiffany. I grew up in Corona, New York, where Louis Tiffany founded a glass company, later called the Tiffany Furnaces. Those mines in New Mexico played out before statehood and most were closed."

"Yes, most."

"What do you mean?"

"It is believed that the mines that produced the Tiffany Blue gemstones included all the *known* turquoise deposits in the basin."

Feeling the challenge, Centori says, "The key to a good story is not who, what, or where, it is why! So why are you telling me all this?"

"There is a legend that one ancient, and unknown, turquoise mine in the Galisteo Basin contains a mother lode of gold."

"Gold—there's gold in them thar hills?" Centori scoffs.

"Mr. Centori, you may find it less amusing when you know more."

"No disrespect. I did come here to meet you."

With a calm stateliness that says that something big is coming, Calabaza continues, "The gold mine is on your land—under the Circle C Ranch!"

CHAPTER 9

CITIES OF GOLD

"**A** turquoise mine with gold deposits on the Circle C?" Centori asks Calabaza with skepticism.

"No one has questioned my word before," Calabaza replies with moral modesty.

"I am sure that's true. Yet, you made quite a statement."

"It is quite a gold mine."

"On the Circle C?"

Calabaza affirms, "Yes, except the lost gold mine is not just deposits, it's a concentration—a mother lode."

"A mother lode?"

"Yes, I come here for that reason, and because this quest is for the strong of heart."

"Okay, where on the Circle C?"

"We don't know, but it would benefit us to agree."

Centori's curiosity piques, "Agree on what, exactly?"

"Tiffany had not found gold in their mines. That could eliminate played-out mines that are close to your ranch."

Centori drains his glass and says, "That narrows it down! No disrespect, but my men are working and I should join them."

"Allow me to further explain."

Centori nods in agreement and Calabaza continues, "Cerrillos Hills is mineral rich, more so than any other New Mexico region, but many minerals are scattered, prohibiting major mining operations, except...I am sure you have heard of the Seven Cities of Gold."

"I do not have the time for myths."

"A myth that led to 16th century Spanish adventurers seeking gold across New Mexico."

"Still a myth."

"The cities of gold were the New Mexico pueblos."

"They were *rumored* to be the pueblos, a legend. A fool's play."

"Every legend has an element of truth, Mr. Centori."

"That is hardly enough."

"The legend is an important element in our history."

Looking unimpressed, Centori replies, "Your story is not easy to grasp. What are you saying?"

"Only six of the seven cities were identified."

"There is no evidence of a seventh city and there is no evidence of *any* city of gold."

"That is true. When Coronado entered New Spain in 1540, he found no gold."

"Then, he moved on. I should do the same," he interrupts.

"No one has ever found or even identified the seventh city."

"I suppose you can."

"Yes. It is near San Marcos Pueblo in the Galisteo Basin, in an area that is now your land. That is believed to be the general location of the seventh city."

"Not a city at all?"

"Ah, you see! It was never identified because it was *not* a city. It was a mine near San Marcos—the closest city."

"If it exists at all. Look, this is fascinating, but my cowboys are working the range."

"It exists, somewhere on your land."

Centori shakes his head, stares and considers a reply, "I'm afraid you dream. You do not know the location of the gold mine, or even if it is real."

"There is a way to find the gold mine."

Turning to the exit Centori moans, "Really?"

"I said that an agreement would be beneficial."

"Yes, you did."

"Mr. Centori, the gold mine is on your land. I know how to find it, but we need each other, a partnership."

"What was that you said about an agreement?"

"Allow me to search your land or join me in the search. You have the door. I have the key. We would share the gold with the pueblo descendants."

"Okay," Centori sighs, "assuming that you have the key, in what proportion?"

Reaching into a pocket for a paper, Calabaza says, "Would you agree to the proportions written here?"

Centori unfolds the paper, reads the agreement, looks up and returns to the paper, "I would agree, but to no avail. Again, you do not know where to search."

Calabaza looks around and lowers his voice, "That is revealed by ancient Indian symbols engraved on an artifact. It shows the location of the gold mine."

"Aha, a treasure map of sorts, but you don't have the artifact. No offense, but I must return to the Circle C."

"There is a story of a pueblo Indian leader and a silver medallion."

Centori shifts, suggesting an end, "Another story or myth?"

Ignoring the skepticism he continues, "The pueblo leader engraved symbols into a Silver Medallion. Then he wrapped the medallion in oiled deerskin and buried it to hide the mine location. If we find the long-lost medallion, we can find the gold."

"Again *if...if* the medallion is real."

"It is real. The medallion remained secret through the Spanish, Mexican and American eras."

"Why was it hidden for so long?"

"The Spanish colonized our land and imposed their ways. Anger led to the 1680 Pueblo Revolt and increased defiance. Fear of the Spanish finding the mine created the secret for future generations. This was not in spite of the crown, but because of the crown."

"Justified defiance against the Spanish crown," Centori concedes.

"The Silver Medallion secret faded with the centuries and was lost to history. The gold was never discovered."

"Lost to history you say."

"At this time."

"Perhaps for all time."

"Do you know Francisco Gonzalo?"

"By reputation."

"Before Tiffany arrived, Gonzalo was researching old mine claims and Spanish Land Grants documents. He discovered obscure references to the Silver Medallion legend. After he told me about it, I was compelled to speak to many pueblo elders."

"Your story is less than persuasive. The medallion has been constantly missing!"

"If you don't understand, please trust me and listen until you do. Our ancestors wanted us to inherit the Silver Medallion and the knowledge contained in the encryption when the time was right."

"When is that?"

"Now is the time. Stories of the legend vary, but stories about the medallion are consistent."

"Why now?"

"The Americans have given up the played-out mines, it is time to find the relic and locate the gold without fear of misappropriation or of any legal challenge."

"We have laws in this country."

Calabaza rolls his eyes, "It is better to discover and distribute the gold before anyone suddenly wishes to *colonize* us again."

"That is far-fetched, but given the history___"

"If the gold vein runs under the old Tiffany mines and not on your land, the company may claim the rights."

"How is that possible?"

"There is legal precedent."

"What precedent?"

"Some call it the law of the summit. Wherever a vein is closest to the surface determines the ownership. If the vein is closest to the surface on the Circle C, you own the right to follow it underground wherever it goes—and the reverse is true! We could resist, but we do not have the power for long legal fights."

"You think it is closest to the surface on my land."

"Yes, but it could be challenged in a court fight, a fight we would probably lose."

"I don't know about that, but you have slim evidence and don't know if the pueblo stories are true."

"I believe in the elders and in the spirits of our ancestors. As children, fireside stories shared by grandfathers attached us to pueblo history, honoring our heritage."

Centori's body language encourages Calabaza, who continues, "We love to listen to the stories of ancient Puebloan customs and traditions. The grandfathers shared a legacy with tales of life-nourishing resources of the pueblos and of how tribal communities marked solar activity, lunar phases and equinoxes."

"Tales you say; I would say the Silver Medallion is a tall tale."

"Consider my reckoning. Over the centuries the Indian stories about the medallion survived, but the burial site is lost to history, until Gonzalo discovered a document suggesting a burial place."

"Why would the Spanish have pueblo documents?"

"Why did the Spanish colonize us at all? The date on the document agrees with the date of the story. They are of the same time period."

Taking the story more seriously, Centori concedes, "Okay, the timing adds up and Spanish respect for the pueblos was lacking."

"Lacking...to say the least," Calabaza adds.

"Does the document indicate where the Silver Medallion is buried?"

"It is a place called *Colina de Agua*."

"Or Hill of Water?" Centori repeats in English and thinks, *Another document that could change the history of New Mexico!*

CHAPTER 10

TURKEY VULTURES

The next morning Adobe Centori awakens at dawn and walks across the large empty bedroom to a washstand. He tips a jug into a basin, stoops down and brings the water to his face.

In the Circle C kitchen, with a cup of very good coffee, he starts to rustle up *huevos rancheros*. The dish—fried eggs on fried corn tortillas with a tomato chile sauce—is his favorite breakfast. He skips the usual side dishes of beans, rice and avocado. Over the meal, he recalls Calabaza's words. *Tiffany mines yielded a quarter of a million dollars a year...Tiffany Blue gemstones included all the known deposits. Yet, legend has it that an unknown turquoise mine in the Galisteo Basin contains a mother lode of gold.*

Centori finishes his breakfast and moves to the horse barn, saddles up and mounts Patriot. He raises his shirt collar against an unusual morning wind and questions why he considers hunting for treasure. The Mexican Expedition decision complicates the matter. Conducting an initial exploration of the ranch could make sense of Calabaza's stories and settle his mind.

More intrigued than he had imagined, he explores the Galisteo Basin near Turquoise Hill. Over the course of his ride, he ranged from Madrid to the east and to Santo Domingo

Pueblo to the northwest. That broad survey of his land showed no promise of the medallion burial site. Instead, it showed numerous locations fitting Calabaza's story. He did not find *Colina de Agua*, but he did find stray calves along the way.

Urging Patriot forward, Centori rides the range back to the Circle C. In the big sky above, two large birds are in dramatic flight. They are buzzards, but they are turkey vultures, whose name is derived from the likeness of its red head to that of a wild turkey. Perched in a cottonwood tree, with spread wings, is another large male turkey vulture; only eagles are larger than this bird. Will he stay or fly away? He flies away, awkwardly ascending with wings shaking and then slightly flapping.

Turkey vultures keep the New Mexico deserts clean by eating dead animals. This important feeding function prevents remains from spreading disease to people and cattle. Although they prefer fresh meat, they are less effective in hunting live animals. Unlike hawks and eagles, their talons are ill suited for snatching live prey. Extraordinary smell and sight senses and flying low to the ground enable the birds to locate carrion. The large birds do not create nests; rather they seek hollow logs or rock crevices within which to nest. They are sure to have more success in their search than Centori had in his search.

With the Circle C Ranch house in sight, Centori stops and looks into the distance as if an answer is beyond the horizon. Then he considers a logic concept in philosophy that of *argumentum ad absurdum*, which is argument to absurdity, used in philosophical reasoning and in debate. This type of argument contains unreasonable or impossible points to prove or disprove a position. *Find a missing medallion that may show the location of a lost gold mine that may exist.*

Out of the blue, a turkey vulture shows its wingspan of over five feet and dives down, curiously close to Centori. The scavenger appears to seek his attention. Then, the bird rapidly ascends and fades away. *Seeing the land through that bird's eyes would provide a great vista and provide a great improvement over horseback... no offense Patriot.* Although the bird is out of sight, Centori's eyes remain fixed on the sky above.

Returning to the ranch, Centori swings down from Patriot in front of the horse barn and walks a path to Little Hill Top. During times of contemplation, he retreats to this Circle C high point. From this point, his view captures the elevations of the Sandia Mountains, the cattle-covered mesas, and the beautiful desert flowers and sage. Fixing his eyes over the great expanse of sky, he wonders, *Where is Colina de Agua? Seeing the land from the sky would indeed provide a great vista.*

Centori bounds down from Little Hill Top and goes directly to the library, where he breaks out several rolled-up maps. He pulls out books on archaeology and geology, and he stacks them on the desk. He knows that pursuing the gold will prevent him from joining General Pershing's expedition. Pushing aside the books in favor of a whiskey bottle, he pours, stares at his acceptance note and rips it up. He is not a day drinker but has a Jameson anyway.

Stepping outside to the blessing of twilight and the setting sun, Centori mentally composes a second note while looking upward toward the sparkling heavens. Back inside and at his desk, the words do not flow. He places one arm on the desk and his head on his arm; it would be easy to fall asleep. Instead, he returns to the task.

After the better part of an hour, and the creation of few drafts, he was satisfied. The message, written with a careful hand, explains why he declines the offer to lead the 5th Cavalry into Mexico. After finalizing the note to General Pershing, he is unsure if he is relieved or disappointed. This story has a conclusion, but not an end.

CHAPTER 11

DEAD WOMEN DON'T
WEAR GOLD

The following sunrise, Centori shares a breakfast with Griegos, "I am going into Valtura this morning."

"Again?" Griegos asks. "Justo?"

"No. I know you are probably wondering about that note from him."

"I figured you will tell me when you are ready."

"I will be ready soon, but first things first. I must make things right between Mady and me. Thanks for not asking about that too."

"You will tell me when you are ready."

Both men laugh and move on to the ranch business.

***

Centori returns to Mad Mady's Saloon to share the gold mine news and seek advice, or to resolve their latest issue. After all, New Yorkers must stick together in the Wild West. He enters the bar. It is quiet. Rose, who is getting ready for the lunchtime crowd, sees him walk into the saloon. Her face changes. He approaches Rose; she is not looking very friendly.

"Hello, Rose, is Mady here?"

"If she were here, I don't think she would want to see you!"

"Okay, Rose, is she here or not?"

"Rose!" Mady calls out from upstairs. "Would you come up and help Sweet Kate?"

"Sure thing, Miss Mady."

Mady and Rose cross paths on the steps.

"Adobe, I didn't expect to see you here so soon."

"Or ever, you may be thinking."

No answer.

To break the mood, she offers, "Do you want a drink?"

"I don't know."

"That usually means you need one," she says with improved decorum from their last encounter.

"No thanks, Mady, you know I'm not a day drinker."

"Okay, coffee. About the other day...your friend probably thinks I am mad."

He does not argue the point as Mady pours his coffee.

Leaning forward over the bar in the empty saloon, she reacts, "I was a little out of control."

"Just a little."

Mady sighs through a smile.

An upstairs woman descends the steps, waves to Mady, and leaves the saloon.

"Adobe. What you don't know about women could fill the Rio Grande Gorge."

"Very funny," he says and flashes a sly smile.

"What is funny is that you are well-practiced in hiding your personal thoughts. There is something between us that remains unresolved, and it may never be resolved."

"Perhaps stealing away in the night requires resolution, Mady."

She shows resentment for the less than tactful remark and replies, "When you tell someone to leave, you cannot be angry when they do so."

"What? I never told you to leave."

"In words, no, you did not. It is unclear what action marked the moment that I decided it was time to leave," she admits. "Except in recent months I felt sad and lost, that was the last straw."

"Mady, I am unaware of the last straw, in words or otherwise."

"And you are unaware of the previous straws too," she quips. "You should listen instead of making inaccurate objections."

"Mady, I couldn't feel worse about what happened."

"Sure, Adobe, but you lost your halo! Time changes everything, except you! You think I don't know why you sit alone in the library for hours. You are not lost in your whiskey. No, you are lost in your past! When you emerge, you treat me with casual detachment. For you the past is not gone, it resides in your library. Oh yes, I know about her photograph."

Gabriela's ghost exists, or he keeps her alive in his head and in his heart. He exaggerates Gabriela in his mind, but illusions can be as important as realities for happiness; she provides direction with influence on his life. At least, that is what he tells himself.

Mady goes on, "Even when you are not in the temple of Gabriela, there is always an indistinct echo of her. Persistent yearning is not an attractive quality. You have been handed so much; your life is both good and abundant."

"Handed, you say?"

Mady nods her assent, but goes on, "Your life is fantastically fine! How wonderful it must be to be you. You suffer no illnesses or insolvencies. You enjoy the beauty of the Circle C. Oh, you are able to love your ranch, your horse and your friends. You love the opera, love your Jameson and cigars—just not me. What about me?"

"That's not true, Mady." He sounds stronger than he intended.

"True enough to hurt."

"Why do you say that?"

"I say it because it is true." Mady drops her voice.

He lowers his head; he has no words.

"*No mas* Adobe! You can make me feel invincible, but too often, you make me feel abandoned. *No mas.*"

"You need not forgive me now, Mady; just forgive me in your own time."

He seemed happy during their first months together, but things did change with time. Mady could feel the ghost, see the ghost in his eyes. It makes no difference that Gabriela is gone these four years. The thought of her still confines him.

Then his face draws tight, perhaps in an attempt to change the subject, "I hope you don't blame me for your sister's death."

She nervously looks down and glances at him, "No, I don't think so...no, I mean of course not. I'm just tired, so tired. The kind of tired you can't sleep off."

"Sharon was an angry and avenging woman, but she was your sister."

"When my sister wasn't on the wrong side of the law, she was on the blind side of the law. I will never understand her cruelty against me."

"You had interesting encounters with her."

He feels his face turning red and wonders what Mady knows. He recovers and replies, "Look, Mady, romance is seldom without challenge." He sips the coffee and goes on, "Sometimes challenges can enhance a romance."

"Perhaps I left the Circle C before you found out that I am really mad."

"I already know! Perhaps it is my turn to be crazy."

Mady nods so slightly that it could be nonexistent, stares and says in an expressionless voice, "Does the last year count for anything?"

The mystery of their dynamic is how they anger and attract each other simultaneously. Whether she accepts him more as a friend than as a lover remains to be seen.

"It counts and now you are back."

"I never left."

She smiles in approval and says, "So who was that man anyway?"

"That's another thing I want to talk about."

***

"What? You're going to search for a lost gold mine?" Mady exclaims. "Adobe, maybe you had some loco weed?"

"Maybe. Please keep this to yourself."

From behind the bar Mady offers, "You will chase a missing artifact that may or may not show the location of a lost gold mine that may or may not exist."

"That's about right, Mady."

"That's a fine state of affairs," Mady flares. "You need to spend time in the Territorial Insane Asylum. It did me a world of good!"

Centori smiles with restraint.

"Did you have that loco weed? You are not a treasure hunter."

"I'm not?"

"No, you are not! You are a successful ranch owner and cowboy," she declares.

"I have been other than a cowboy before."

Declining to be impressed, she says, "If I didn't know better, I would say you are doing this for Gabriela." *But dead women don't wear gold*, she thought, yet she would not say it aloud because he would do anything in Gabriela's defense.

Even though Mady spent more than a year at the Circle C, she did not exorcise Gabriela—a ghost that never stopped living, a ghost he never stopped loving. He raises his brow and is silent, unwilling to react. She notes this with some satisfaction and goes on, "I didn't mean to say that."

"It is fine, Mady. Guess I am still sensitive about a lifetime love."

"You didn't spend the rest of your life with her."

"No, but she spent the rest of her life with me."

"Look, you don't need to do this. Your ranch is financially sound and beef prices are currently at record highs."

"Mady, why do you assume this is about me?"

Puzzled, she shifts closer and says, "What are you saying?"

"It could be my destiny to discover this lost mine. If it is on my land."

"You are not one to adhere to legends of buried treasure or lost gold mines, Adobe, be reasonable."

"It's not unreasonable to believe that the lost gold mine might be found and, if it is found, the gold can improve the pueblo communities and New Mexico."

"I see it in your face, the determination. It's a longshot, but you are resigned to be unreasonable."

"No. I am resigned to help the pueblos and the state."

"I see, and it does your heart good."

He hesitates as if weighing his response and then says, "The trouble is a missing map of sorts. I know it sounds foolish."

"Then why chase it? However well intended, this is not your responsibility. If anything, it is probably fool's gold. I have seen some from the basin right here in my saloon. Why chase a wild goose?"

"I have my reasons."

"I thought it was sentiment that drives you, Adobe. I didn't realize how much until I came to the Circle C. I understand and accept one simple fact."

"And what is that, Mady?

With a note of empathy in her tone she states, "You hope that she will somehow find you again."

Centori makes no response.

CHAPTER 12

REVERT REDEMPTION

Mady was close in ascribing motive to Centori's desire to find the gold mine. While Gabriela does not motivate him directly, the U.S. violation of the Treaty of Mesilla and his action concerning the Revert Document influenced his interest in the gold.

Feeling responsible for the treaty violation, finding the gold could somehow ease his conscience. If Gabriela had not been his opponent in the Revert Document affair, she would be alive today. Had he not been so determined to violate the treaty and achieve statehood, they would be together today. In the current case, the gold will go to the rightful owners; he would not be hiding something and controlling destiny. Unknown to Mady, the gold could be redemption for his questionable actions connected to the Revert Document. Centori is ready to find out.

"I am sure you have your reasons. You are no stranger to making impulsive decisions."

"Mady, the decision is made. The gold can help the pueblo people and make the valley and New Mexico a better place."

"The existence of this gold mine has been known for centuries, and now, all of a sudden, they present it to you? Don't you find that a bit curious?"

"I do, but I have been persuaded. Beyond the story, the challenge is hard rock mining, where gold is extracted from enclosed rock."

"You can find mine workers, if you need them. Provided that the Silver Medallion is found," Mady insists.

"Yes, of course. This search could return that history to the pueblo communities, after a long record of Spanish colonization and domination."

Ignoring the lesson, Mady smiles, "Of course you have been swayed. You have a weak spot when it comes to helping people."

"I don't think so, Mady."

"Oh, you don't think so. Ha! You are Adobe Centori and you go where you are needed."

Centori smiles slightly, blue eyes pleased.

"You are a great New Mexican," she says, then thinks, *but not much else when it comes to me.* He stares at Mady's Navajo jewelry as if it is a sign to assist Calabaza in finding the gold mine.

"Thanks, Mady."

Now, Centori must send the refusal note to Pershing as soon as possible.

CHAPTER 13

SOMEWHERE ON CIRCLE C

The next morning, Centori is ready to confide in Griegos about the Calabaza meeting. In the kitchen, he rustles up coffee and brings a cup into the library seeking geological information.

A cup later, there is a knock on the front door.

"*Buenos dias*, Boss."

"Francisco! How about some coffee?"

"That's why I came," he jokes.

Centori waves him to the kitchen, where he pours the hot brew into two cups. They take filled cups and sit around a large rectangular table.

"If you don't mind me asking," Griegos pauses, "is everything all right with you and Mady?"

"It is as good as it can get."

Griegos receives an answer as coffee scented steam comes from his cup. He takes a sip and remarks, "Good coffee."

"At least I'm good at something," Centori's voice drops.

"What are you talking about?"

"After careful consideration, I have decided not to accept General Pershing's offer. I have arranged for a telegram to be sent to him."

Griegos drops his cup to the table and says, "That is good news!"

"My decision is not without some regret."

"I'm sure of that, but you have done more than most for Uncle Sam. Besides, you are needed at the Circle C."

"Thanks. Pershing has no idea how long he would pursue Villa, or how deep into Mexico he would go to find him. The expedition will probably take months, if not longer, with no promise of success. Besides, fighting a guerilla war with a regular army is next to impossible."

"All good reasons," Griegos says then raises his cup, "*Salud!*"

"I have been distracted from ranch business. Thanks to you and the boys, the roundup is moving along."

"We have good news about the roundup. We have run down just about all the mavericks and have a record number of new calves wearing the Circle C brand."

"Good work, as always. Hope you boys know how much I appreciate their work."

"They know."

"I wasn't much help this year."

"It's not every year that a big general calls you for a meeting."

Centori smiles, "Right, and it's not every year we look for a gold mine!"

"What?"

"Francisco, I call upon our friendship and iron-clad trust."

"Of course; you have my trust without reservation."

"Remember that note from Justo Calabaza?"

"Yes."

Centori pauses for a sip of coffee then confides, "He said there is a lost gold mine somewhere on the Circle C."

"On the Circle C?"

***

An informed Griegos reacts to Centori's explanation of Calabaza's proposal, "That is an unbelievable story."

"A story that depends on finding the Silver Medallion, if it exists," Centori replies.

"I don't put much stock in legends."

"There could be gold here, but I just don't know how much."

"If anyone were foolish enough to try to find it; this is a big ranch."

"I need another fool to join the search and share any gold that is found. What do you think?"

Griegos holds the cup up with two hands and answers, "Besides that finding it is doubtful, old mines should be left alone. There are many hazards in exploring neglected mines—they can be damned death traps!"

"This search carries some risk," Centori agrees.

"Some risk? Without more information, it might be impossible to uncover the medallion. Even then, there is no guarantee that it can point to a lost mine."

"Can I take that as a yes?" Centori asks.

"As long as we find the gold before the fall roundup, two fools are better than one."

Both men laugh and Centori says, "I know it's a longshot."

"A longshot is pulling an inside straight. We need a prayer!"

Centori offers a smile, a handshake and three words, "*Colina de Agua*. That's unusual in the high desert."

"That's right. It could be some kind of a code."

"I am sure that is not enough of a clue to find the artifact."

"We need more," Griegos agrees.

"Besides, things change over time."

"Especially over centuries."

"Let's go take a look at the map."

Returning to the library, Centori rolls out a map and points, "The Circle C is a big ranch and the medallion could be anywhere."

"We have to look beyond *Colina de Agua* to see what we are missing."

Griegos takes a deep breath, looks down at the map and repeats, "A lost gold mine somewhere on the Circle C."

"Yes, well, maybe. We can read a map, use a compass and guess what *Colina de Agua* is telling us, but let's see Justo together. Perhaps we can figure out something. I have another meeting set up."

"Fools rush in where angels fear to tread," Centori quotes.

CHAPTER 14

BEEF STEAK GOLD STAKE

Close to 5:00 p.m. Centori and Griegos mount up and ride to Valtura at a relaxed pace. Along the six-mile road from the Circle C to town, Griegos questions the validity of Calabaza's claims. Although the ride and the natural beauty are familiar, the riders explore the terrain with a fresh perspective.

Arriving on National Street, they pass the *Valtura Journal* newspaper office, now owned and operated by the *Albuquerque Journal*. Turning right on First Avenue, they tie their horses in Valtura Plaza. Adjacent to the *Valtura Journal* is the Union Hotel on East Corona Street and First Avenue.

Entering the hotel restaurant to an aroma of roasting chiles, desk clerk James Clarke greets them, "Good afternoon."

The two men nod in return and move to the usual corner table. Both men sit with their back against a wall with background noise of forks and knives rattling faintly. The service is always fast.

"What can I get you, Sheriff?" Janie asks over the sound of voices.

Centori did not seek reelection for Corona County sheriff, but old habits die-hard.

"I'll have a Jameson."

"And for you, Francisco?"

"The same thanks."

"Right away."

One minute later, the drinks arrive. Ten minutes later, Calabaza arrives. After an exchange of greetings, he says, "Mr. Centori. I hoped not to widen our agreement, no offense to your friend."

Griegos nods his acknowledgment.

Centori rapidly reacts, "This is Francisco Griegos. Anything that concerns the Circle C concerns him. Besides, we can use his help."

"You have my discretion, if more can be told to me," Griegos adds.

Calabaza takes the vacant chair. Centori waves to Janie. She returns and takes orders: beefsteaks, cooked in various ways. Papitas, pinto beans or frijoles and green chile are the side dishes. Calabaza orders a beer.

"Now you both know we seek a lost gold mine. This story is in old papers and in the old stories of the pueblo people," Calabaza reviews.

"*Las Siete Ciudades de Cíbola*," Griegos says.

"Yes, the legendary Seven Cities of Cíbola; cities of gold sought by the Spanish in the 16th century."

"If I recall correctly, the viceroy of New Spain sent Coronado and his men to search for the cities. According to legend, the seven cities of gold were in the pueblos of the New Mexico Territory," Griegos states.

Two men enter the restaurant and walk by their table. Griegos has a sip of whiskey, waits a moment and goes on, "They traveled from Mexico into New Mexico and never saw any city of gold. Instead, they found Indian Pueblos, which may have inspired the false legend. Coronado returned to Mexico on a route that later became the Royal Road."

"As discussed with Mr. Centori, no evidence of a seventh city was ever found."

A lively debate ensues about the existence and interpretation of the Seven Cities of Cíbola. Some ten minutes later, Janie returns with a large tray and serves the men. They pick up their drinks and wait then she asks, "Anything else for you gents?"

"No," Centori smiles, waits for her to leave and interjects, "There is still the issue of a Silver Medallion."

With his elbows on the table, Calabaza leans forward, "Yes. We have a mystery to solve. That is true."

"Another truth is that more information is needed to solve the mystery," Centori adds. "Now, it is a fool's errand."

"We will have guidance," Calabaza counters.

Centori places his knife and fork down and declares, "You are accepting too much on faith with too little information."

"You agreed..."

Centori cuts into a succulent steak and says, "I have not broken my word. It's just that we have too much muddle. Without the Silver Medallion, we are done before we begin."

"Perhaps we would be making history."

"Let's not get ahead of ourselves," Centori replies clearly unimpressed.

"Mr. Centori, you seem to have changed your position."

Centori lightly brings his fist down on the table and recites, "No, but we need more to start the search. Not everything that glitters is gold. We could be making a big mistake. The search is almost sure to fail."

"Almost, you say?" Calabaza asks.

Slicing another juicy piece of beef, he answers, "We have the low cards now. Too low to start a search. It would be a useless undertaking. Right now, you have narrowed down the area to a big part of a big ranch."

"As I told you, we have a meeting with Gonzalo; he may have a winning hand."

"I don't know him," Griegos says.

Janie comes over to check on them. The men smile and focus on their beef until she leaves.

"Gonzalo, who has experience in mining, told me about the Silver Medallion. He is a rancher, a miner, and he has a very beautiful woman," Calabaza informs.

Centori nods and flashes a small smile, "Yes, you mentioned Gonzalo; he may have clues or relevant documents."

"Gonzalo will do his best," Calabaza says, and then has the last of his beef.

"He may have to do more than his best," Centori adds.

"Perhaps old maps pinpoint the location of old mines," Griegos says.

"For a mine that has no observable reality," Centori replies returning to his beefsteak. Nevertheless, a *troika* consisting of Adobe Centori, Francesco Griegos and Justo Calabaza is formed.

CHAPTER 15

RATTLESNAKES AND BATS

Centuries of New Mexico mining history are reflected in places named for the industry, such as Silver City, Golden and the Turquoise Trail. The mineral enriched Cerrillos Hills, north of the Circle C Ranch, contain silver, copper-manganese, iron and gold.

Francisco Gonzalo managed mining operations during the turquoise boom including three gold mining claims in the eastern part of the Cerrillos Mining District, called the San Marcos Pueblo Grant. His sheep ranch *Rancho de las Aquila* adjoins the mining district, which his father owned and is on the *Camino Real* in the *La Cienega* Valley south of Santa Fe. In earlier days, the ranch was a *paraje* for those traveling to Santa Fe on the *Camino Real*. Strategically located, the ranch provided trade goods for travelers and a good place to rest and to trade stories.

Rancho de las Aquila has Spanish colonial structures built in the early eighteenth century. Standing in the portal of the main house that dates from the Mexican period, Gonzalo looks from under a handmade embroidered *sombrero* and declares to his visitors, "There is not enough gold, if any, in the played out mines."

Calabaza turns to Centori and Griegos then says, "How can you be sure?"

The men had arrived after spending the morning in the saddle. Rather than taking the Atchison, Topeka and the Santa Fe from Valtura, passing through Lamy, and riding a spur line to Santa Fe, they decided to survey the land on horseback.

"You know that I worked those mines in the Galisteo Basin. I don't believe they contain enough gold," Gonzalo answers. "Perhaps enough for placer mines. I'm not even sure of that, but certainly not at the levels you expect. The Silver Medallion legend is interesting, but to me, the artifact is not a serious indication of a gold mine."

Calabaza feels an impulsive objection to the word choice and says, "The medallion is mentioned in some of the Spanish Land Grant documents."

Gonzalo takes a deep breath and asks, "Do you have any experience in geological or mining engineering?"

They do not.

He reacts to the silence, "I didn't think so."

"We need to find the artifact first," Centori interjects, "and we thought you would have maps from the Spanish era that could provide clues. As Justo said, documents indicate that the medallion is buried in a place called *Colina de Agua* or Hill of Water."

"Excuse me for a moment," Gonzalo answers.

As the three men wait, Centori notices a pack of Marlboro Red Tip cigarettes that sits on an outside table. It reminds him of another person who smoked that brand, a person who is watching him now.

"Here you are gentlemen." Gonzalo pushes the Marlboro pack aside and rolls out an old regional map. They scan the chart. After a moment of consideration Gonzalo states, "Nothing extraordinary here. Nothing that suggests *Colina de Agua*."

Calabaza reflects, "Water in our arid environment is elusive. The first civilizations emerged near rivers, taking sustenance from the water. The people of New Mexico made their villages and farms near river valleys, where there is enough water for survival."

"*Was* enough water for survival. Keep in mind that water drainage can be selective. Erosion may have followed many unknown paths over the years," Gonzalo suggests. "Pueblo, Spanish and American people irrigated the river valleys by sidetracking water into canals that were often washed away by high water during the spring."

Centori points, "Here, look at this, two small streams flow apart and then together."

"Yes," Gonzalo says, "Tributaries of the larger stream."

"From the Rocky Mountains, the Rio Grande flows south through New Mexico," Griegos thinks aloud.

"If you allow me, I would like to borrow this map," Centori states.

"I trust that you would return it in good condition."

"You have my word."

"Then you may borrow it, and you may consider my advice. Assuming you find the medallion, it may not provide enough information. Keep in mind that some old mines are covered with loose rock and are hard to see. Others may have caved in and look like ground depressions. That is just the beginning. The alleged gold mine that you seek is probably underground. Beware of certain factors in exploring underground mines. Perhaps I should give you all some tequila while we talk."

There are no objections.

A few moments later, the men hold generous glasses of the distilled blue agave drink.

"*Salud*," Gonzalo offers.

"*Salud*," the others echo.

Gonzalo continues, "Consider that the discovery of valuable minerals in the earth is filled with challenges. A fault line can alter a vein, with the lost part of the vein relocated if not completely lost. We may need a professional geologist to find the split part. The vein may have dropped to an excessive depth or may have moved to the surface and eroded away." The other men stare at him and listen. A woman stares down from a second story window and listens.

"Understand that fault problems are complex, particularly if the appearance of the rocks was changed by metamorphic action. Beyond locating the mine, a challenge is in excavating the hard ore. That could require the extraction of gold ore through tunnels or mine shafts."

The woman in the window is stark naked, but as composed as a Renaissance nude. She is riveted on the conversation below.

"For a decline or tunnel, a box cut is needed as an entrance," Gonzalo informs as he notices movement in the upstairs window. "The quality of the bedrock must be accessed for safety. A vertical shaft drilled near the ore is another option, if gold ore is confirmed."

In a strange fashion, the woman above draws closer to the window to view all the men.

Gonzalo drains his glass and warns, "You want to restart a dormant mine; there are risks and hazards that can kill." He takes another deep breath, "Do you even have any experience in entering an abandoned mine?"

They do not.

"I didn't think so. You seem to have the sand and the spirit, but you should consider the danger."

The woman above draws even closer to the window, flapping curtains slightly hitting her naked breasts.

Gonzalo offers, "Shall I pour another?"

They all agree.

"Once inside an old mine you must be cautious about six key dangers. One, assume that any ramshackle support structures will collapse. The deeper you journey, the greater the danger. You could encounter cave-ins and drops at every turn. Two, it is vital to treat every formation with restraint. Be on the alert for large rocks that look unstable. Your movements could disrupt the rocks."

Gonzalo removes his hat, dries his brow and begins to enjoy sharing his knowledge. "Three, watch out for open shafts and extraneous holes concealed by dim lighting and containing water; watch for drainage. Four, be mindful of poor ventilation or bad air—that will be obvious. Five, do not touch or inspect any abandoned equipment. You could be embracing explosives, dangerous chemicals or become entangled in wire."

"We hope you will supply equipment," Calabaza says.

Gonzalo reacts, "Before that, have you considered hiring experienced men?"

"We have not," Calabaza answers.

"You asked about equipment," Gonzalo says, "You will need a metal detector to find the medallion. If you find the mine, you may need dynamite, but try to rely on drilling. If you are lucky, the pathways will be clear. I can outfit you with what you will need to carry. Then there is the issue of gold extraction, a procedure needed to extract the gold from its ore. You may need a combination of methods in mineral processing, if you ever find the mine."

Centori glances at his partners before asking, "You said six dangers."

"Oh, yes. Watch out for rattlesnakes and bats."

CHAPTER 16

MAIOLICA VASE

The naked woman in the window quickly dresses and rushes downstairs. From under a flat hat with round brim, she confronts Gonzalo, "Who were those men?"

"Friends, just visiting."

Seething through a smile as if accepting the answer, she stresses, "Do they have names?"

"You seem upset. What's wrong?" His remark had anything but a calming effect.

As gloomy as a rainy day in a cemetery, she demands, "Who were those men?"

"Men of the Circle C Ranch and one from Santo Domingo Pueblo."

"I knew it—Adobe Centori!" she roars.

"Yes. Centori, a well-known respected man."

"A well-known what?"

"He is a big ranch man in New Mexico."

"What was he doing here?"

"I told you, a friendly visit."

"That's not what I heard!"

"I don't know what you think you heard."

"I heard enough."

"Why are you so angry? Do you know him?"

"No. I never met him."

"Then the visit is not your concern."

She rapidly retreats a few steps and fixates on a vase. It used to be a fine Renaissance Italian Maiolica vase. The red earthenware clay pottery had an opaque white glaze over beautifully painted designs. Now it is a broken mess scattered at the feet of Gonzalo.

"*Eres una mujer loca!*"

She offers a strained laugh and sneers, "If I were you, I would stop talking, or should I show you my mind?"

"*Bruja,*" Gonzalo yells as a matter of fact.

Solana's eyes become as blank as a cloud covered sky. Looking as angry as she feels, she raises her fists to challenge the sky above and storms away. Hell has no fury like Solana Bejarano.

CHAPTER 17

SOLANA BEJARANO

Solana Bejarano's dramatic clash with Gonzalo was extreme. Their usual fights are mild by comparison. Perhaps too much Chimayo Whiskey, bourbon with rare New Mexican mountain herbs, fueled her fury. She would argue that seeing Centori was enough fuel.

Last night, she hosted a celebration at *Rancho de las Aquila*. Since her arrival, a year earlier, the ranch is known for sophisticated, sparkling fiestas with spectacular music. As a fabulous host, she led the guests around the floor in a variety of New Mexico folk dance patterns. The irregular turns represent the winding journey of life, especially true for her.

In her late thirties, Solana stands at five feet, six inches, with brown eyes and dark brown hair. She loves to wear her figure about Santa Fe Plaza. When they met on the plaza, the much younger beauty with a slender body and full bosom immediately attracted Gonzalo. She is a demanding woman and found him easy to manipulate, like her previous men. The art of self-promotion, an ability that she has mastered, is enhanced by her dangerous nature.

Solana addresses Gonzalo in an inflated loving way, designed to take something. At the same time, she acts as though taking advantage is far from her mind. It takes one look at Solana to understand her power, his acceptance and their dynamic. Beauty and a rapacious sexual appetite are the reasons she has a prominent position at the ranch, and the reasons why he tolerates her extravagant spending on expensive furnishings.

Silver candlesticks, antique Spanish boards and writing chests are part of the ranch. A luxurious *trastero* cabinet is filled with expensive tin-glazed earthenware plates. The furnishings arrived despite his request not to fancy up the place. Wool-on-wool embroidered *colcha* adorns her bed. The ranch is well stocked with many fine wines, except French wines. Her adverse reaction to all things French remains a puzzle to Gonzalo.

Solana embraces the Mexicanidad movement and rejoices in many things native to Mexico, especially formal attire, and claims to descend from a Spanish colonial family. He accepts her shaky story for fear of losing her affection, but he is less accepting of her smoking of Marlboro Red Tips.

Gonzalo rules the ranch in important issues, but she has made a significant mark. Adept in the role, she plays her hand well and is well entrenched at *El Rancho de las Aquila*. Solana Bejarano can be crude, cruel and cutting, but extremely affable and approachable, which softens his opinion—every time. Yet, his forbearance is limited. She smokes, drinks and is heartless. She is as cold-blooded as a rattlesnake. She could not love a man if she tried.

CHAPTER 18

COLINA DE AGUA

Back at the Circle C, the three men examine Gonzalo's old Spanish map, hoping to find something they missed. Centori says, "The original document indicates that the medallion is buried at *Colina de Agua*, or Hill of Water."

"Yes, that's right," Calabaza agrees.

"Gonzalo said there's nothing extraordinary on this map. We can see there are no waterfalls or big rivers or anything that could be considered a *Colina de Agua*."

"Hmm, no big rivers," Griegos says and points to the map, "Something about how these two small streams flow apart and come together."

"Yes, tributaries of the larger stream," Centori adds. "Francisco, wait! What was that you said about centuries?"

"Things change, especially over centuries."

"Yes, centuries of erosion. Hmm. That could mean some places have been reduced in size, rock and soil moved away by water and wind," Centori calculates.

"It takes thousands or millions of years for that kind of substantial change, not just centuries," Griegos says.

"True, I'm no expert on erosion rates, but geological forces could change water courses over centuries. At the time of this map, the tributaries and the stream could have been called *Colina de Agua*. The pattern could be dried arroyos now."

"I see your point," Griegos says.

"Yes, something about the way the water runs around what could be a hill," Centori repeats. "There is something extraordinary on this map!" Centori bangs his fist on the table, "The two small streams which flow around and form the larger stream could be the arroyos around Little Hill Top!"

Griegos face lights with a smile and he says, "That's right. It sure looks that way."

"The artifact might be buried near this previous rich water supply with a hill breaking up its flow—*Colina de Agua*," Centori declares.

"I see," Calabaza agrees, "Except this map does not show a hill."

Griegos adds, "True, and Little Round Top does not have any water supply, but geological forces could have changed these water courses."

"We don't know, but it is a good place to start a fool's errand," Centori observes. "My instincts say that *Colina de Agua now* is Little Hill Top."

Griegos nods and says, "Then the Silver Medallion is near the Circle C Ranch house."

"Fools rush in where angels fear to tread," Centori repeats.

"Let's not rush in without a metal detector," Griegos jokes.

CHAPTER 19

LITTLE HILL TOP

Vicente Conrado rides to Albuquerque to purchase shovels, spades and a metal detector. Centori visits Little Hill Top and considers the possibilities of being close to the Silver Medallion. The land feature is the Circle C high point, three hundred feet behind the ranch house.

The next day, minutes before sunrise, Centori, Calabaza and Griegos move single file along a dried arroyo toward Little Hill Top. First light peeks over the Sandia Mountains, illuminating the house, the front portal and the dramatic vigas.

As the sun clears the top of the Sandias, the men stand on the crest of Little Hill Top. With lots of water on hand, they pull on gloves and start to excavate. Centori and Griegos use spades for digging and scraping, shovels for scooping and lifting to work through hard earth, rocks and small cactus plants.

The diggers work downward within a five by five foot square, level by level. Calabaza uses a trowel for close work. Then he moves the metal detector over the earth that was shoveled to the edges of the square before pointing the metal detector over the hole in the ground. Beeps reveal nothing except broken copper tools and arrowheads. He repeats the process with the metal detector that has a range of two feet.

During a water break, they are silent. The Circle C men exchange glances of frustration before they resume work. Calabaza remains stoic.

The painstaking work continues as fatigue takes its toll. Centori and Griegos switch from leading with their left side to their right side.

At high noon, with shaky and sore muscles, the Circle C men return to ranch business. Calabaza returns to Santo Domingo Pueblo. The Silver Medallion remains a legend.

On the second day of excavation, the men return to the work site and resume the search. They find a rhythm that spends energy efficiently and limits movement. Using their entire bodies minimizes stress to one part of the body or a single muscle. Digging and scanning reveals nothing except a few pottery shards with thick lines and hints of heavy glaze.

At 11:00 a.m., they climb up out of the hole and end the work earlier than planned. Griegos sums up the day's work, "*Nada.*" Discouraged, but not defeated, the team rests and will be ready for another day.

That night Centori sits in his library with almost every part of his body aching from the day's work. Jameson provides the appropriate remedy.

On the morning of the third day of digging, Centori drops his shovel in frustration and says, "We couldn't find this thing with a search warrant. A trained archeologist couldn't find this medallion. I would have had better luck finding Villa with Pershing."

"What was that?" Calabaza asks.

"Nothing. I am done for the day and maybe for good."

CHAPTER 20

STORIES OF LUNACY

Solana enters Mad Mady's Saloon wearing a *rebozo*. The long, narrow flat shawl handwoven with a fringe, wrapped around her upper body, expresses her secret Spanish identity. Shortly after her escape from prison, she confronted Mady about betraying Centori. Mady said no. After learning that Mady was at the Circle C, she saw it as a way to seek revenge on Centori. Mady again said no. This time she can provide incentives.

The saloon is closed, but not to the striking Spanish woman who loves to make an entrance. She breezes though the doors and waits. Mady sits and works at her table. Rose McFie is behind the bar cleaning up. There is some activity upstairs. While Santa Fe Sharon is unrecognizable to Rose, Mady immediately jumps up. From across a long saloon room she exclaims, "Sharon! If I knew you were coming I would have baked a snake!"

"Calm down, Mady. My name is Solana. Sharon, as most people believe, is dead."

"What the hell are you doing here anyway?"

"Nice to see you too and nice to see you kept some of my French decor."

"You are crazy to come back here."

"Look who's talking. Perhaps madness runs in our family."

"You are supposed to be dead!"

"I'm very much alive."

"Damn, I said what are you doing here?"

"It must be my intense nature in desiring to see you."

"If you are recognized you could be returned to prison, not that I would care."

"Mady, I am your sister and I have come to help you."

"Help me! You have never done anything to help me! Quite the opposite!"

"Sister, when everyone thought I was dead, I sent you a message so you would know that I was alive."

"You sent me to the Territorial Insane Asylum. I was almost killed! Damn it, what are you going to tell me now?"

"It's what *you* are going to tell me about your precious Adobe Centori."

"What, him again? What drove you to this obsession? How does your mind bring about your criminal behavior?"

"Oh my, Sister, so many questions."

"But no answers."

"What can't be cured must be endured. I assure you it's nothing too serious."

"You have never been a good liar."

"You don't believe me?"

"Not for a second."

"Then don't! Look, Mady, in time I will make things right between us. Can you wait?"

"If I believed that, *when* makes little difference. Sharon, I am sick of hearing stories contrived through your lunacy."

"I told you my name is Solana and they are just stories."

"Are your delusions and suspicions just stories? Is your obsession with Adobe just a story?"

"Calm down, Mady, you are hysterical. Who is detached from reality? Besides, you say that as if it is a bad thing. Everything has value. When the value changes, everything changes."

"What do you value?"

"I value myself," Sharon declares.

"That has not changed and that's why people don't like you."

"I don't blame them, Mady, but I may blame you. You share a bed with him."

"No. I left him and the Circle C, so don't even tell me your plan."

"Oh, is that right?"

"Yes, so end whatever you want now."

"You are still close enough. He trusts you. It will a perfect revenge for his..." Sharon stops short.

"Not sure what you mean, but I am sure you are wrong!"

"I mean to help my sister."

"The hell you do!"

"You still love him?"

"I will praise the day I stop loving him." Mady reflects, "We have problems...what can I say about him?"

"Enough to fit on his tombstone," Sharon taunts.

"I will not help you!" Mady screams, "Are you trying to exact some kind of price from him?"

"Calm down, Sister, you are hysterical."

"I am calm, but you are a disturbing mystery, more brave than clever."

"Not such a bad thing. Those traits have served me well."

"Have they?"

"Mady, you are my sister!"

"I wish I were not."

On the upper railing, the upstairs women do not react; they are rankled but outwardly indifferent to the sisters and move away. Another woman moves closer to the stairs and listens.

"Why can't you be happy living your lies with Gonzalo on his ranch?"

"Some scores need to be settled, Mady. I will have my revenge on Centori."

"It was not enough revenge for you in burning down his horse barn?"

"That was an accident. I can leave that fool Gonzalo and make things right between us."

"Just how will you accomplish all that?"

Sharon looks at Rose and says to Mady, "Send her away."

"Why?"

"Because what I am about to say is just between sisters."

Mady shakes her head from side to side, but calls out, "Rose, please go get the morning newspaper."

"Sure, Miss Mady."

Rose leaves the saloon as an upstairs woman moves even closer. A few seconds later Mady stares down Sharon and says, "Okay, what is it?"

"We can make things right between us with a gold mine."

"What gold mine?"

"Who is detached from reality now, Mady? I can see it in your face. He told you! I knew it!"

"I don't know anything about a gold mine. You better fix your temper, Sister."

"Perhaps, if you wait long enough, I might."

"Seek your revenge if you must, but remember if you dance with the devil, one day the music will stop."

"Nice sentiment, Mady. Don't bother to deny it, I overheard Gonzalo and Centori at my ranch and I want more information."

"I told you, I don't know about any gold mine."

"Have it your way, Mady, but keep it to yourself and don't warn your highly skilled lover."

"Highly what?"

"That's right, Sister, he had his way with me while you were locked away in the looney bin. Some romantic hero...Ha! How does it feel?"

Hoping this is a lie, Mady grimaces and asks, "What do you mean?"

"I mean that I got your man upstairs in *your* big beautiful bed!"

Mady is shocked into silence. Sharon continues her cutting remarks, "I was naked in his arms___"

Mady interrupts forcibly, "Why would you say that?"

"Because it is true."

"Go to Hell! Don't worry it will only feel like an eternity."

"Sorry, but when I want something I give it my all, I'm funny that way!" Sharon replies without sympathy.

"Why, damn you!"

"Remember, you got most of mother's money."

"You are lying about him."

"Oh, really. Why don't you ask your doves about your honorable gentleman, that special wonderful man. Ha!"

Mady makes fists and moves closer to Sharon, then stops and covers her face with her hands. Her vivid racing mind forces her hands to close again.

"How does it feel?" Sharon taunts. "He was not raised by saints!"

"You better leave," insists an enraged Mady.

"If I leave, I may never come back."

"If you don't leave now, I won't want you to."

"Listen to reason, Mady. He is a no good fornicating engine."

Mady, a volcano about to erupt, yells, "I'd rather listen to the devil!"

"You don't believe me, ha! You look at me as if I am not your sister."

"I think you are not. Who are you?"

Sharon, fueled by anger and determination states, "I'm your loving sister."

Devoid of any emotion except rage, Mady says, "I have never hated you more than right now."

"Oh, Sister, you don't mean that. I love you."

Still seething, Mady says, "What kind of love drives you down destructive paths? What kind of madness drives you to steal my saloon, to kidnap me and throw me into the crazy house?"

Sharon, who believes in vengeance, declares, "We are all a little insane."

"You seduced the man you knew I loved!"

"Then you believe me! Sister, he is not much of a man."

"I'm going over to the hotel. I expect you to be gone before I return."

"Mady, you are naïve. No one is good; no one is a hero. You just can't see it, but I can see through it all!"

"You see it all through cold eyes. One more thing. You are dead to me."

Sharon, who is prepared to do anything including humiliating her sister to achieve her ends, replies, "I am not excessively concerned."

"You are mad."

"That's something I would not know about."

"Well, I do *and* I have never known it more than right now," Mady adds as a parting shot. Rose stares from behind the bar and Sharon returns a crazed look that quickly ends the stare.

Sharon stops to measure the situation around the bar and scans the empty room looking for an audience. Then she looks up at an upstairs woman who summons her. After a moment of deliberation, she gently grabs the lavishly carved *balustrade* and gracefully ascends the stairs.

CHAPTER 21

CARMENCITA

At the top of the staircase, Sharon arrives into a smoke-filled hall that has hazy lighting and a few women of easy virtue. Mady's upstairs women wear ruffled petticoats, bright bows, silk stockings and garters. Sharon is distracted by voices from nearby rooms, no words, just voices. Then a beautiful woman greets her, "*Buenos días señorita ven bonitos.*"

"You think so?"

"Yes."

"I *do* look beautiful! Do I know you?"

"*Soy Carmencita*," she says with a smile reserved for certain women.

"I am Solana."

Allowing no time for small talk, she says, "You don't have to hide the truth from me, Sharon."

"What?" While not intimidated, Carmencita's brashness is surprising, "My name is Solana!"

Two laughing women enter the saloon and climb the stairs. When they see Carmencita, their faces become expressionless and unconcerned.

"What do you want anyway?" Sharon says in a voice with an edge of resentment.

"This is not the right place to talk. Let's go to my room."

Sharon hesitates and glances down before returning her eyes to the mystery woman, but she accepts the request. They enter one of the small bedrooms. The curtains are drawn. An oil lamp is on a chest of drawers and a bed, which takes up most of the room, is in a corner. Carmencita closes the door and declares, "I know who you are!"

Startled by the exposure, Sharon struggles for a reaction, "And who are you?"

"A woman as beautiful as you."

"Yes, if my imagination is better than my eyesight," Sharon says with a mocking voice.

"Are you sure you wish to insult me? I know your secret and your game with Gonzalo."

In an angry voice, Sharon replies, "You don't know what you are talking about!"

"Oh, I believe I do know. A woman in my position hears many things."

"You mean overhears, don't you?"

"What's the difference?"

"How do you know Gonzalo?"

"News like that travels fast," she quips.

Sharon stares into the eyes of her host, seeking a better answer.

"It is more than just hearing things. I have seen things with my own eyes. You see, *Senorita*, I attended one of your fancy fiestas at *El Rancho de las Aquila!*"

Sharon, frozen as if she did not hear the comment, finally says, "I don't remember you!"

"I am sure Gonzalo would remember me."

With a confused look Sharon says, "You desire to threaten me?"

"Not yet."

"I am leaving."

"There are reasons why you should reconsider. You have a very good situation at *El Rancho* and with Gonzalo. He can replace you with very good women for his bed."

"What?" Sharon yells out.

"Rather than engaging in matching our hot-tempers against each other, would you like to know why I called you?" Carmencita asks calmly.

Casting her eyes sideways with more wrath than words, she declares, "Not particularly."

"I'll tell you anyway," she says with a wicked smile. "You seek gold!"

In a distressed voice, attempting to mislead, Sharon says, "What are you talking about?"

"Ha, now you know how Mady felt a few minutes ago."

"There is more to it than gold. To give you confidence in me—you seek a lost gold mine and revenge on Mady's friend Adobe Centori."

"Who are you?"

Remaining quiet for a few awkward seconds, and then smiling as if complimenting herself, she then says, "I told you, I'm Carmencita."

"How do you know all that you say?"

"So it is true!" she smirks.

To show herself as a ferocious and fearless competitor, Sharon moves very close to her antagonist, "You are pretty sure of yourself for an upstairs woman!"

If anyone except Mad Mady dared to criticize Carmencita, there would be a price. Yet, she ignores Sharon's comment.

She takes her eyes away for a moment until Carmencita says, "Mady could return soon; you better go out the back to avoid her. I enjoyed our talk."

Somewhat baffled, Sharon prepares to leave and says, "It was *less* than talk!"

Carmencita smiles, moves even closer and adds resolutely, "You will return once you think it over. Besides, with so much involved, I should have you in my sights. *Hasta pronto. Adios,* Solana; goodbye, Sharon."

CHAPTER 22

RECONCILIATION

Mad Mady, depleted by the Sharon encounter, sits alone at a table in the Union Hotel restaurant. Janie comes over and asks, "Are you checking on the competition, Mady?"

"No, just taking a break."

"Everything all right across the plaza?"

"It will be."

"Sure Mady, what can I get you?"

"A whiskey please...and Janie."

"Yes, Mady?"

"Thanks."

Mady sits nursing her drink and her contempt for her sister. Since Sharon's escape from prison, Mady tried bribery and threats to protect herself. Knowledge of an escaped felon places her at risk. Yet, turning in her sister seems unthinkable—until now. Yet, the only way to reconcile the competing pressures is to keep Sharon away.

On the way out, Mady sees Janie and whispers, "If you ever want a job at Mad Mady's Saloon..."

"No thanks, Mady."

"I meant a downstairs job only!"

"Of course, I know. You take care. Whatever your trouble, it too shall pass."

Returning to the saloon, Mady goes upstairs and feels someone on the steps behind her; she turns to see Sweet Lady Kate reporting for work.

"Good day, Miss Mady," Kate offers.

Mady ignores the greeting and moves rapidly down the hall. She unlocks her door and enters her room, still processing Sharon's unhinged behavior and lies, especially that lie about Sharon in her bed with Centori.

Disturbed, Mady stares at that bed and sits on the edge. Then she rolls onto the bed, face up with her hands doubled into fists. She bites her lower lip to no avail. Within seconds, the upstairs women standing in the hall hear muffled, agonizing sobs. Deep in her heart, she knows there is some truth in Sharon's claim.

An hour later, Mady emerges from her room to an array of inquiring eyes. Anguish apart, she walks past the women and toward the stairs, her eyes level and straight ahead. As she reaches the staircase, Sweet Lady Kate articulates what the others are thinking, "Are you okay, Miss Mady?"

With her pride intact, she replies, "Just fine, Kate."

Mady descends the stairs as Rose comes out from behind the bar and gently asks, "You all right, Miss Mady?"

"Yes, of course—more than all right!" Mady answers with head high and eyes damp with tears.

"That's good Miss Mady," Rose says in support.

"Now, let's get back to work."

With all the dignity she can summon, Mady walks to her table and tries to process a simple truth, but the truth is seldom simple. In any case, Mad Mady Blaylock is back in business!

CHAPTER 23

ELEMENT OF TRUTH

Despite Centori's misgivings, he unenthusiastically agreed to continue the search for the Silver Medallion. Therefore, the men continue their labor on Little Hill Top. Because of their frustration, each day's work was shorter than the previous day's work. Today, the men work the shovels, trowels and a metal detector, hoping for better results. Their hopes are dashed.

Centori looks at Calabaza and declares, "I'm sorry, Justo, but this is the end of the trail."

"It's just another bad day," he says.

In a thoughtful voice, Centori adds, "After bad *days* there is no rhyme or reason to continuing digging."

"I can feel the artifact under foot!" Calabaza implores.

"I'm sorry, but if this hill eroded over the centuries, the medallion could have been exposed and washed away."

"That's right, Justo, it could be anywhere," Griegos agrees and shakes his head.

In an attempt to prolong the discussion, Calabaza says, "We could chart out a system."

"Without the medallion? That is beyond a longshot!" Centori replies.

Pointing on the map before them, Calabaza claims, "We could start here at Mount Chalchihuitl and continue the search by moving inward toward the center of the ranch."

Griegos responds, "Mount Chalchihuitl is the oldest turquoise mine in New Mexico, but there is too much land to cover without the medallion."

Centori adds, "Even with the medallion, which could narrow down the search area, the mine entrance could be obscure. We don't have the medallion; we should end this foolishness."

Griegos comforts a dejected Calabaza, "Justo, we tired our best."

"This is a dead end," Centori says throwing his shovel down in frustration. It hits an object yielding a metallic sound. The men stare at the tip of the object. Calabaza quickly digs with his hands to free the object—he holds up a round metal object buried for centuries. The men marvel at the find and carefully inspect what appears to be an old pendant. Perhaps it is the Silver Medallion; any leather strip and the oiled deerskin are long gone.

Calabaza gently removes centuries of earth with a small brush; the artifact comes into focus. It may contain a valuable secret, marking the location of the lost city of Cibola. Overcome with emotion he says, "Remember, every legend has an element of truth, Mr. Centori. This appears to be the Silver Medallion!"

CHAPTER 24

SILVER MEDALLION

Inside the Circle C library, the men are aware of the potential enormity of the Silver Medallion—if they can understand its meaning. Without asking, Centori places the medallion on his desk and pours celebratory whiskey, however premature. Three men surround the artifact, down whiskey and absorb the impact of their discovery. They stare at the engraved design as if it will scream a meaning. It does not.

Calabaza picks up the piece with piercing eyes riveted on the relic. The others wait hoping that he can read the symbols. They do not wait long for his interpretation. "The engravings appear to be the mountain ranges around the Galisteo Basin," he announces.

"Are you sure?" Centori asks.

Ignoring the question, Calabaza points at the medallion, "Based on the relative positions of the symbols, these are the Sandia, Jemez and Ortiz Mountain ranges."

"That makes sense," Griegos says. "There were operational gold mines in the Ortiz Mountains."

Centori adds, "Yes, the early Spanish conducted placer mining in the Ortiz Range. They discovered gold veins. In fact, it was the first lode in the West, but low grade ore and lack of water closed those mines."

Griegos asks, "Should we begin our search there?"

"No," Calabaza replies quickly, "The medallion indicates two other mountain ranges and there are other important signs." Returning to the medallion, he continues, "The swirling circles represent the Rio Grande. However, look here...in the middle is a shape of a fetish bear that could be life-sized."

"Life-size fetish bear?" Griegos questions.

"Fetish symbols, small stone carvings representing culturally important animals."

"Right, but what do you mean life-sized?"

"Could be a rock formation is shaped like a very large fetish bear. It could be a large stone carving or rock arrangements and the entrance to the mine. In pueblo ceremonies and pueblo mythology, a bear cave helps us contemplate our consciousness. Some bears may be hesitant to leave the cave and enter the sunshine after hibernation."

"The gold mine has been in a long state of hibernation," Griegos imagines.

Calabaza nods, "People can return to a cave to regain a state of peace they had before."

"Are you saying we could have the peace we had before this search? We should forget the whole thing?" Centori retorts.

"No, not in this case. I am not. I believe the bear was engraved for a reason."

"We come out of the cave into the sunshine and find the gold mine," Centori contends.

"Or we enter into the cave for the sunshine," Calabaza counters, "with the gold being the sunshine."

"Very interesting, but we still need to find it," Centori adds.

"Do you see the heavy lines here?"

"Yes," the others acknowledge.

"They indicate mountains intercepting light rays, casting long shadows changing the landscape appearance. We enter the shadow and see the bear."

In reaction to puzzled looks, he goes on, "The medallion suggests that at a certain time in the afternoon shade, the outline of the fetish bear becomes prominent—it is revealed!"

"So you think the gold mine is located at that point," Centori states.

"At the bear, near the bear or in the bear cave," Calabaza reasons.

"How do you know that?"

"I don't know that, but I believe the artifact says find the bear and we will find the entrance to the mine."

Centori pours another round of drinks before stating, "Even if you were right about the bear, we don't know its location. I have been riding this range for years and have never noticed a bear rock formation."

"You never noticed the bear, but it could still exist."

"I know this range too," Griegos adds, "I have never seen a rock bear, I have seen Camel Rock in the Espanola badlands, near the Tesuque Pueblo."

Centori adds, "We have all seen the large chunk of weathered sandstone that looks like a camel. It's about 40 feet high and hard to miss."

"The fetish bear is probably man-made," Calabaza says.

"Man-made or naturally weathered, I have never seen a bear," Centori contends. "We are far from finding the mine," Griegos adds.

"Not so far," Calabaza says. "You know the lay of the land, but that is not enough. Looking south from San Marcos, the Sandias appear with this angle, suggested by the heavy engravings. We should look to the afternoon shadow when the mountains look red from the west."

"What about this corn image?" Griegos asks.

"This corn figure suggests the beginning of the growing season or harvest season."

"Growing season is right about now. Okay, where does that leave us?" Centori inquires.

"In the middle...look at the outline of a fetish bear."

"Outline?" Griegos asks.

"Yes, in a rock formation, visible in the late afternoon from the west. When the Sandia Mountains turn bright red we look at the shadows cast over the basin."

"When the Sandias turn a watermelon red," Centori echoes.

"Yes, from the north we see shadows fall upon the rock formation. The outline of the bear could be recognized, perhaps only from high ground as seen from the Jemez."

Griegos shakes his head and says, "That may narrow the search but it is still a vast area."

Centori looks at the medallion and repeats, "It is a vast area and we could easily miss the bear."

"It could take weeks with no promise of success," Griegos states.

"We need to take to the air," Centori states as both men look to him in confusion.

"Justo, you think the bear can be seen from the Jemez. Yet, that would be impossible to see from such a distance, and as one gets closer, it is less likely the bear is visible. Is that about right?"

Calabaza nods in agreement but qualifies, "It would only be possible to see the bear from high ground and great distance with a signaling plan."

"Which we know nothing about. We should take to the air for a bird's eye view!"

CHAPTER 25

EYE IN THE SKY

Barnstorming pilots who perform aeroplane exhibitions are growing in popularity. Sometimes called a flying circus, barnstormers travel through America to engage the air and the enthusiastic crowds. One such pilot is the sister of Centori's statehood constitution colleague. Her name is Carlene Cortina. She lives in Santa Fe, but the exhibition circuit takes her to Albuquerque.

Known for her aviation skill in distance, durability and aerobatic maneuvers, Carlene Cortina is the fifth American woman to obtain a pilot's license. In addition, she is one of the first women to carry airmail for the U.S. Post Office.

After a telephone call, Centori and Cortina agreed to meet late in the afternoon at the Territorial Fairgrounds in Albuquerque. Most barnstorming takeoffs and landings are on dirt, gravel or grass fields. The horse race track on the fairgrounds provides the needed surface and space. Cortina arrives to an awaiting Centori. She is wearing leather headgear and a jumpsuit. Although her clothing is more practical than stylish, she is attractive.

"Thank you for this, Carlene."

"Well, I did promise you a ride in the air. In fact, I thought I did not make a good impression in Santa Fe."

"You made an excellent impression in Santa Fe. It was a demanding time, but we wrote the state constitution and achieved statehood. Your brother was a good ally in the process, and a good friend for introducing us."

"I am kidding. How are you?"

"I have been busy with the spring roundup. In fact, this search will confirm that all calves are accounted for and end the roundup."

"Sure thing, Adobe. Any questions?"

"No, but here is a map of the Circle C Ranch."

"I see."

"Can we cover this area while flying low?"

"I'll do my best," she smiles.

"Thought you are a barnstormer," he teases.

"Okay, we will fly as low as safety allows," she replies while handing him a pair of goggles and headgear.

"Thanks."

"No problem, barnstormers carry extra equipment in preparation for any contingency. By the way, meet Jenny."

"Who?"

"My aeroplane. The JN-4, built by the Curtiss Aeroplane Company. See the open topped number 4 that looks like a Y?"

"Oh, yes."

"So, the nickname Jenny!"

They climb into Jenny's open cockpit, she starts the engine, the propeller comes to life and the plane shakes. Soon after, she receives the takeoff signal; he receives a wave of anxiety. Then throttle up. She pulls on the stick. He pulls himself together. The light plane accelerates. They lift off.

Centori's first flight is alarming and exhilarating. The sensation of rushing air sweeps them into the great wide-open sky. The propeller settles down to an obscure whirr. He views the beautiful blue skies over the high-desert landscape and marvels at the sight of the Circle C Ranch below. In every direction, the seemingly endless, wide-open range of splendor and inspiration is before him. Consumed by the enormity of the experience, he forgets the purpose of the flight. From this lofty perspective, he thinks, *What a beautiful sight.*

Out of the huge blue sky, two hawks appear in the distance and then alongside the plane, yards off the wing tip. Centori acknowledges his escorts with a nod and wonders how they are able to keep up. Seconds later, they are closer as if saying, *now you get it.* They seem to be allowing him into their world as an authentic flyer.

Cortina follows the flight plan that covers the area within the three mountain ranges. She starts at the Ortiz Mountain foothills. He stares down at the terrain looking for the fetish bear. When she rolls toward the Jemez foothills, the mixture of open land and mountains create strong winds. Centori is startled, but one glance at the cool Carlene Cortina calms his nerves.

From the Jemez she banks the plane and heads to the Sandia foothills. Suddenly, a swirling upward moving gust of air, a dust devil, takes control of the plane. A wild ride ensues. She turns into the gust, slowly eases back on the throttle, charming the stick back. Easing in the little flap, she decreases the forward movement before she takes control and flies away from the turbulence.

"Are you okay?" she yells above the noise.

"Sure, why wouldn't I be," he smiles nervously, concealing his anxiety.

Completing the coverage of the basin with concentric circles and narrow circumference, she begins crossing the inside area within the triangle of ranges in arranged patterns. As they circle above, he looks below for anything that could resemble a fetish bear.

For more than an hour, flying as low as possible, he strained to see the bear, to no avail. Then she turns and stares, "Are we done?"

"Okay, we are done," he yells.

She signals an acknowledgment, banks the plane and heads back to the Albuquerque Airfield. The return ride is as smooth as silk, allowing Centori to focus on the highly talented, beautiful woman sitting in front.

On the ground she removes the leather headgear, flashes a smile and shakes out her hair, "We circled the triangle of mountains. Were we successful for your purpose?"

"It was a great experience, I can see why you love flying," he evades.

"Did you confirm that all your mavericks were rounded up?"

Caring less about a cow than a bear, he answers, "Yes, I did. I did not see any mavericks except a great pilot. It was a success. That was a fantastic ride."

"Glad you enjoyed it...are you willing to throw caution to the wind again? I mean come up with me again."

"Only with you, Carlene. For now let us play it safe on land. How about a meal at the Alvarado Hotel?"

"Wonderful, let's take my motorcar."

They enter her Studebaker Speedster. She is again chauffeuring Centori, but this time on land.

"This is a great looking motorcar," he compliments.

She accelerates and shouts, "Welcome to the 20th Century!"

CHAPTER 26

ALVARADO HOTEL

In 1902, the Alvarado Hotel opened its doors on First Street in downtown Albuquerque. The outstanding hotel is the focus of Albuquerque's social and political life. The mission-style building has red roof tiles, bell towers, fountains, and has a remarkable large lobby with carved beams and huge fireplaces. The restaurant, parlor and reading room are first class. In addition, travelers can shop in stores for Indian jewelry and blankets.

The railroad hotel is part of the Harvey House chain. Fred Harvey created restaurants for the Atchison, Topeka and Santa Fe Railway. The servers, called Harvey Girls, are single, attractive, and smart young women of good personality. They wear modest black and white uniforms with their hair tied with ribbons.

Carlene Cortina and Adobe Centori enter the Alvarado Hotel lobby. "This is quite a place," she says appreciating the Spanish and Indian decorative detail in the lobby. Then, the flying duo enter a black oak paneled dining room. A fine-looking Harvey Girl escorts the fine-looking couple to a table.

"Yes, it is a remarkable hotel and this restaurant is first rate. First time for you?"

"I have traveled here by rail, but not dined in here. I take it you have been here before?"

"Yes, I have attended the annual reunions of Spanish-American War veterans here," Centori states.

"Oh, my brother said you are a war hero."

"I don't know about that, but I know that we have had two presidents speak here. TR, as he likes to be called, came in '03 and he gave his speech on a platform right out front."

She edges her chair a little closer as he continues, "Taft came in '09 and did the same. Statehood was a big issue at that time. Of course, he signed the statehood bill on January 6, 1912."

"You witnessed those presidential events," she smiles admiringly. "I understand you were among the New Mexico contingent to witness President Taft sign the statehood bill."

"Yes, that's true. I did go to Washington and now I witness another great event right now at this table."

Taken off guard, her only response is a flash of uneasiness. After a Harvey Girl takes their order, she says, "Would you like to tell me what we were looking for today?"

Now he is off guard, but answers, "As I said, mavericks," he replies with something else on his mind and in his face.

Unsatisfied, she signals with her eyes that she wants more.

"As usual, the Circle C Cowboys performed their work pleasantly and thoroughly."

She places her right index finger to her chin, "Really?"

"Well, Carlene, you welcomed me to the 20th Century. I may be the first cowboy to conduct a roundup from the sky!" he says hoping to change the subject.

Her shoulders go up and down. "Hmm, mavericks. I could believe that, if you wish."

"I wish to enjoy this time with you," he replies in an attempt to cloak the bear, "Enough talk of my work. Let's talk about you."

She smiles, looks around and says, "I love this place. I enjoy fine things: art, poetry, music, food and love."

Somewhat taken aback, he replies, "I see that you love to fly as well."

"Yes, I feel free in the sky. The air up there in the clouds is very pure and fine, bracing and delicious. Why shouldn't it be? It is the same the angels breathe."

"That is beautiful, Carlene!"

"Thanks, but I can't take the credit. Mark Twain said it first."

"Still, coming from you it sounds beautiful."

"You have a way with words, Mr. Centori!"

"I don't know, but I like to keep my word."

"You speak with veracity, and say what you mean almost all the time!"

"You don't believe I was searching for cattle?" he says as a form of admission.

"As I said, I could believe that, if you wish. You must have reasons for secrecy that have nothing to do with me."

"Yet, you are curious."

"Oh, so I am," she says with a smile, "Besides anything you say to me is in the direction of truth."

He nods in agreement, "Yes, of course."

"Knowing you is like flying. Sometimes in the air, I don't always know where I will go...I spread my wings and determine which way the wind is blowing."

With a semblance of a smile, he tries to take the comment as a compliment, and then she abruptly says, "Is it true that Mady Blaylock has left the Circle C?"

"What?"

"Did I startle you?"

"Guess news from Mad Mady's Saloon travels fast in Valtura."

"Even to Albuquerque. Mad Mady is widely known. So is it true?"

"It is true," he confirms without giving more information.

"I see you waste no time seeking the company of a woman."

He does not respond.

"Do you love flying with me?"

"Yes, Carlene, very much. I like being with you, even when we are not in the air."

"Oh my. You are quite the romantic," she asserts.

He presents a big smile. She let his words hang in the air before asking, "Do you want another woman in your life?"

The question is able to disturb and comfort him. He recovers enough to offer her another drink, but that's all.

***

They drive back to the airfield in her fancy car. Centori leaves his aviator friend with regret. The impact of her bright eyes remains as he envisions kissing her. He does not know when he enjoyed a woman's company more, but then he remembers. As is the case with life's great moments, their day together ended too fast.

CHAPTER 27

CIRCLE THE TRIANGLE

That night inside the Circle C library, Centori informs his partners about his aeroplane ride, "We covered the area and saw nothing that resembles a fetish bear. It is just not visible."

"Well, at least you had an air ride with that pretty lady pilot," Griegos says.

Centori smiles and corrects, "You mean Carlene."

"Yes, I do."

Calabaza interjects, "The bear was not visible to you."

Centori stares and says, "That's right, not to me or anyone else who would try."

"You did not see it," Calabaza says rhetorically.

"I told you, the air search revealed nothing."

"Yet, it could be revealed."

"How is that possible? We conducted an extensive search."

Griegos interrupts, "You still insist that the bear exists? He just failed?"

"You are forgetting one thing," Calabaza declares. "The corn image on the medallion suggests the planting or the harvest season. Planting begins in April and can continue to June. The harvest is October through November."

"That depends on your interpretation of the medallion," Centori replies. "We agreed that it is a reasonable risk to start now. That should not have affected our search too much."

"Remember, the heavy lines on the medallion indicate mountains intercepting light rays, casting long shadows. It suggests that at a certain time the landscape changes to reveal an outline of the fetish bear. The shading of objects is perceived in relation to other objects. Contrasts vary with different views. That would explain the failure."

"Failure?"

Centori and Griegos exchange feelings about the comment with their eyes.

"It could have been anyone's failure."

"The bear is difficult to see, as intended."

"What?" Centori says as more of a protest than a question.

"The light source and shading cast upon the fetish bear can appear as a different shape or no shape at all, depending on the season."

"Wait a minute," Griegos calls out. "Contrasting shadows can change an object but how much?"

"Enough to prevent the wrong seekers from finding it."

A confused Centori says, "Only shadows during the harvest season would reveal the bear?"

"Not exactly, but it helps to be a true believer."

"You wish to fly above and see what I did not," Centori challenges.

"No."

"Yet you agreed to an air search," Centori shakes his head. "Are you trying to convince us to go back to land navigation? We *all* failed at that, Justo!"

"We have been successful in learning that the Silver Medallion engravings appear to be the Sandia, Jemez and Ortiz Mountain ranges. Swirling circles represent the Rio Grande and the heavy lines indicate shadows. In the middle is a rock formation that is like a fetish bear. We must manage each part of the puzzle as it is presented."

"Another puzzle? Perhaps the bear was not meant to be found," Griegos says suggesting that it may not exist. "We seem to be going in circles."

They stay silent for a few seconds, sensing an impasse. Then Centori utters, "Going in circles? There was something Carlene said about the triangle of mountains."

Calabaza nods with encouraged and remembers an ancient ritual.

"In times of trouble, the Navajo formed circles around a coyote, banged stones together while taking steps to close the circle. The trapped coyote would become scared. Then the people stepped away, opening the circle to allow the coyote to choose a path of escape, providing an important sign."

"Yes, we should take a step back from the bear—Carlene said we circled the triangle."

The others wait for more, but Centori pauses for a moment, and says, "If I am mad enough to continue, we must be systematic—take a step back and think in terms of a triangle of mountains within a larger math system."

Calabaza and Griegos look at each other.

"Mady might be right. I should enter the Territorial Insane Asylum for not ending this now."

"You mean *State* Insane Asylum," Griegos corrects, "but what is this about a math system?"

In the far distance, a coyote who is outside the circle howls in agreement with Centori.

CHAPTER 28

CENTROID

Centori sits alone in the Circle C library with a Cuban cigar, Jameson whiskey, a map of the Galisteo Basin and the Silver Medallion. His *sanctum sanctorum* is a good problem-solving venue for addressing ranch business and political problems, and complications stemming from love. Despite his doubts, he intends to solve the fetish bear mystery—if it exists at all.

Earlier in the day, Centori began to read the *Albuquerque Journal* story on the Mexican Punitive Expedition. Before finishing the article, he tossed the paper aside and attended to important ranch business that served as a distraction. Now, back in the library, he reads about what could have been his adventure. General Pershing is about to launch his expedition into Mexico. The *Journal* updates Pershing's progress in preparation to capture revolutionary leader Pancho Villa.

He places the paper aside as his thoughts return to the fetish bear. *Interesting pueblo mythology. Calabaza said that a bear cave helps contemplate consciousness. Some bears are hesitant to leave the cave and enter the sunshine after hibernation. Perhaps I should return to the cave and forget this issue. I have been riding the Circle C range for a long time and I never saw a bear rock formation. Even from Carlene's aeroplane, no bear was visible from the sky.* Pushing away his uncertainties in favor of the Jameson bottle, Centori pours whiskey and gazes across the library to a wall of books.

Chasing Cibola was unsuccessful in the 16th century and remains so today. Perhaps the Silver Medallion is as useless as a meaningless symbol in a mathematical formula. Since Centori gave his word to Calabaza and by extension the pueblo people, he will try another approach to locate the bear.

Centori moves to rough-cut bookcases and scans a certain shelf until he finds an old mathematics textbook. Pulling out the dusty volume from his New York University days, he will combine legend with science. He recalls that math articulates the movements in the universe, provides an expression of its forms and explains all things from atoms to stars. With that power, mathematics could easily find a rock formation in the middle of a mesa.

Using a mathematical formula requires an understanding of its principles. It does not take long for him to remember the centroid of the triangle. Next, he must identify parts in the formula that relate to the engravings on the Silver Medallion: the three mountain ranges. He starts with the map of the Galisteo Basin and identifies key topographical areas.

The surface basin's main watercourse is the Galisteo River, which flows from the east into the Rio Grande near Santo Domingo Pueblo. Covering about 450,000 acres, it ranges from San Miguel County in the east into Santa Fe and Corona counties in the west. The Sangre de Cristo Mountains rise in the northeast, as do the Sandia Mountains in the southeast.

Located between mountains and linking the Rio Grande Valley with the Great Plains, the Galisteo Basin was a trade route. Native peoples and Spanish conquistadors explored the region. Centori will do the same.

Studying the Silver Medallion engravings and the corresponding map, he draws a triangle, connecting the three mountain ranges: Sandia, Jemez and Ortiz.

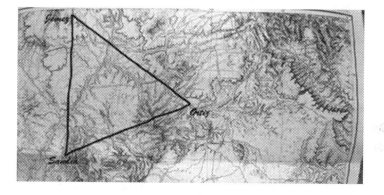

Returning to the textbook, he identifies an appropriate formula that could determine where the bear is located: the centroid of the triangle. He puffs the cigar over the textbook, *The centroid is the average position of all points in the coordinate directions.* He takes another puff and studies an illustration of the centroid of a triangle.

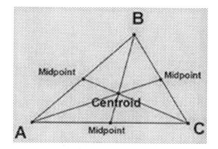

The next morning, Griegos, Calabaza and Centori reconvene in the Circle C kitchen over a pot of pitch-black coffee. Centori begins, "I said I need a system." He points to a book sitting on the table and goes on, "We can find that system in here."

"What is it?" Griegos asks.

"A mathematics textbook. I have a formula that could solve our problem of locating the bear."

"You mean to say mathematics can find the gold mine?" Griegos questions.

"No, but it can help find the bear. From that point, we are on our own. It's a strategy worth following. Remember, the medallion indicates that the bear is somewhere in the center of the three mountains. We can significantly narrow down the search area with this mathematical formula."

With looks of skepticism, they wait for more. Centori taps a page in the book and says, "Understanding the properties of a triangle will provide a valuable clue to our mission." Using his finger to trace a triangle, he says, "First we identify points of a triangle called medians. Here, here and here. Then, viewing the three mountains as a triangle, we can locate the center of the mountains."

Holding their coffee cups, Calabaza and Griegos look down at the textbook.

"How do we apply this relationship to the bear," Griegos contemplates.

Centori slides his finger to each vertex and continues, "The medallion shows a triangle determined by the mountains. If we find the center of the triangle or the centroid, we could find the bear!" Centori informs.

"Sounds too simple," Calabaza says.

Centori thinks for a moment, "Simple in concept, harder to apply to the open range. We need to find the intersection of the three medians of the triangle formed by the mountains."

The others take coffee, focus on Centori and wait for more.

"Now here is where it gets interesting. Each median connects to a vertex on the opposite side of the triangle."

"A vertex?" Calabaza asks.

"Yes, a vertex of an angle. The endpoint where two lines meet. Look at the lines here. The medians run through the centroid and divide the area of the triangle in half."

Calabaza stares at the page and says, "I don't see an application to a vast area of open range."

Centori taps the page again, "Look at this drawing. The medians are concurrent—the point of concurrence is marked G—or the centroid!"

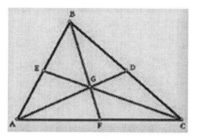

"Find the centroid and we could find the bear," Griegos observes.

"That's right. Let us say this ABC triangle represents the three mountains engraved in the Silver Medallion with vertex A, B, and C. We need to find these midpoints, E, D and F."

"In the wide open range?" Griegos questions.

"Hold on," Centori points at the drawing. "Here...F is the midpoint of AC, E for AB and D for BC. The crossing of these lines, the intersection, is only at this point." He firmly places his finger over the point on the illustration, "And that point is G."

"Find point G and find the bear," Calabaza confirms.

"Or close enough to conduct a sensible search."

"Okay, Boss, now what?"

Instead of answering, Centori reaches for the coffee pot and fills their cups. The more he explains the centroid's symmetrical beauty, the more optimistic he feels about finding the bear.

"Cowboys are great at riding the range," he states. "Think of the positions of the Ortiz, Jemez and Sandia mountains—that's our triangle! We have three men and three sides to this mountain triangle. I will ride from the Jemez to the Sandias, Francisco from the Sandias to the Ortiz and Justo from the Ortiz to the Jemez."

"We all know that range and the basin," Griegos says.

Centori, who is convincing himself that the centroid will work, nods and turns back to the page, "If we plot our mountain triangle, then from the Jemez to the Sandias is AB, from the Sandias to the Ortiz is BC and from the Ortiz to the Jemez CA."

"That could work," Griegos says.

Centori glances at the men and continues, "Using the foothills as start and stop points, ride in a straight line whenever possible. Remember, think of drawing a triangle with lines from the Jemez to the Sandias, from the Sandias to the Ortiz and from the Ortiz to the Jemez. Record the time of the ride. When you arrive at your stop point, turn around, retrace your path and ride half of the recorded time."

Griegos reaches into his saddlebag, "Here are the stakes and red flags, with one set for a backup." He hands out the markers.

"Now, at that point, stop and place a stake in the ground with a red stake—that will be our medians, Centori continues, "From the medians, we ride at a designated time and in calculated directions to the opposite vertex until we cross paths—intersecting lines. The point where two of us intersect is the general location of the gold mine. The third rider should cross at that point. That will place us roughly at the centroid where we should find the bear."

"Or close enough to conduct a sensible search," Griegos repeats.

"Yes," Centori agrees. "We go to our marks at 3:00 p.m. and start at a slow gallop."

"What if we miss each other?" Griegos asks.

"Fire a shot every 30 minutes to signal our approach and watch for our dust. We don't want to miss each other."

"Sure, if we are aware of our *bearings,* finding the bear will be as easy as a Sunday afternoon," Griegos quips.

CHAPTER 29

BEDEVILED

Carmencita arranged for a corner room on the top floor of the four-story Union Hotel. The small and charming room, with furniture of reasonable quality, faces away from the plaza. It is one of Valtura's finest hotel rooms. A secret meeting arranged for high noon will provide the privacy required to announce her intentions. She removes a bottle from a case and places it on a small table near the small bed.

Carmencita moves to the window to look upon the town and the mesa beyond, anxiously awaiting her guest. As the time ticks away, she wonders if her guest will show up at all. There is a strong knock on the door. She swings open the door with a flair and says, "Nice to see you again."

"We will see," Sharon replies cynically. She could not afford to ignore her.

Carmencita smiles, "Come in. How was your journey?"

She struts through the threshold and replies, "Pleasant enough; too many men on the train trying to know me."

"Sorry to hear that."

"I am used to it," Sharon says with satisfaction.

"Sit down."

"I don't have much time."

"Why? Will Gonzalo question your absence?" she says in a rather unkind voice.

Sharon answers, "He will not, but why seek my attention? Why do you bedevil me?"

"Why so angry?"

"I don't get angry, I get suspicious. What do you expect of me?"

"It is not a case of expectation; must I repeat certain things? *Conozco tu juego con Gonzalo y la situación en su rancho. Atendi a una de sus elegantes fiestas.* It's simple, Sharon, you will take me as a partner."

"Partner?"

"Yes, a business arrangement."

"Stop being evasive."

"*Si senorita.* If you agree, I will leave Valtura, never to return."

"Agree? Why would I care if you left Valtura?"

"Yes, agree to share the gold as partners."

"What gold?"

"I told you I hear things."

"Not sure what you heard, but I am sure that you are dreaming."

"Go ahead, have it your way and risk your position at the ranch."

"I am not worried," Sharon snaps.

"Of course not. Gonzalo would forgive your deception. After all, beauty forgives many sins."

Sharon smiles in agreement and Carmencita continues, "Yet, *un vaquero rico* like Gonzalo can have many women."

Sharon, in check, says, "What do you want?"

"As I said, a business arrangement. We find the gold mine together."

"If I don't agree?"

"Your secret will be revealed to Gonzalo. He may be kind and just throw you off his ranch or he may have you arrested."

"If I agree?"

"Then, I will go to Los Angeles and never return to New Mexico. All I want is enough gold to be fancy and respectable in California."

Without a suggestion of irony, Sharon asks, "Are you sure there is enough gold for that?"

Carmencita stares and makes no reply.

"What makes you think I know anything about a gold mine?"

"So you lied to Mady about it?"

"What I say to my sister is none of your business."

Without anger, Carmencita whispers, "We shall see about that."

"No one takes our conversations seriously," Sharon says louder.

"I do."

"My sister will not help me."

"Do we need her?"

"What if we fail?"

"Then I will never speak of this again and you will keep your position with Gonzalo."

After a long stare, Sharon offers her hand in agreement. Carmencita ignores the offer and hugs her for more than a few seconds.

"What was that?" Sharon says in protest.

"Was it bad?"

"I was not expecting that; any further attempts at familiarity will be repelled."

"You expected to be the aggressive one? You are not as ferocious as you sound."

"You wish to tame me," Sharon snarls.

"I am not a beast of prey, but I can tame you and not cause you the least bit of unhappiness," Carmencita replies tartly.

"We shall see. I have seen your face before."

"Yes, Sharon, you have in the mirror. We should have some tequila."

"How can I trust you?"

"Have a drink and know me better."

"You want more than a business partner."

"Now you are getting to know me. Beyond working at Mad Mady's Saloon, I do not seek the company of men. I depend on women for companionship. You may feel the same way given your arrangement with Gonzalo."

"Are you so sure? Are you jealous of my situation or just my beauty?"

"I admit that your appearance makes me furious."

"Do you mock me?"

With a change of manner, Carmencita says, "No, I am attracted to you."

The flattery disarms Sharon who signals less resistance.

"Shall we drink to our new partnership and another for our new friendship?"

"I suppose so."

"Good, all at the same time. Lucky for us I have a bottle."

"Ha...lucky? It is positively uncanny."

After several drinks of tequila, Sharon returns the embrace.

"You held me exactly the way you appear," Carmencita observes.

"What?"

"A hungry look leads to a hungry embrace. I knew you would come to your senses."

"Yes, just enough sense to leave."

"Leave?" she says with a malicious look.

Sharon makes no reply. Carmencita goes on, "You cannot treat me this way."

"I must return to the ranch; the old man will begin to miss me. Besides, we had drinks to our new partnership."

"What about drinking to our new friendship?"

"I made no such promise."

"Those who have challenged me have made bad choices and have paid a price."

Carmencita takes on a look of contempt, very different from her previous expression of seduction. Sharon takes on an unnatural look that is somewhat disturbing.

"You are insane?" Carmencita demands.

"Perhaps insane enough to consider staying with you," Sharon retorts while opening the door and leaving the room.

Carmencita, enraged by the rejection, paces the room. Sounds come from the other rooms. Footsteps cross the hallway and move from hearing. The murmur of voices, then quiet. She waits for what she is hoping to hear, the sound of Sharon returning.

Less than a minute later, Sharon returns roughly and without reservation. More concerned about protecting a secret than being intimate, she declares, "We do have more to discuss."

"*Te gustaría tequila?*"

"*Me encantaría eso.*"

Carmencita smiles seductively and pours the tequila.

Sharon returns the smile and without saying a word lights up a Marlboro Red Tip.

"Is this so unusual for you, Solana?"

"No, just unexpected."

Halfway through the bottle of tequila, Carmencita stares into Sharon's eyes like a killer wolf finding its prey.

"*Mucho major.*"

Sharon does not remember if she returned to protect her secret or to know her potential paramour better. Is it practicality or primitive instincts? Halfway through the bottle of tequila, it does not matter.

Carmencita approaches and drops her voice to a whisper, "It will not be a frightful night."

"I returned to discuss our plan, nothing more."

"Yes, of course, but first things first."

***

Later in the evening, Carmencita states, "You are not such dull company after all."

Sharon's reply lingers between puffs of smoke. Then she says, "Now you will be more inclined to protect my position at the ranch."

CHAPTER 30

ANGLE ALLIANCE

As the sun reaches its zenith and dominates the vast New Mexico sky, three men at the Circle C Ranch engage in a final briefing. Standing next to their horses, they are ready to ride the range and find the medians on the sides of the triangle of mountains. Top cowboy Vicente Conrado will be in charge while Centori and Griegos are away.

"If we start now, our timing should work. Ride in a straight line as much as possible from your start position and record the time of the ride," Centori recounts.

Griegos continues the confirmation, "Sandia to Ortiz in a straight line is about 20 miles, Ortiz to Jemez is about 38 miles, and Jemez to Sandia about 32 miles. When we arrive at our destination mountains, we turn around, ride half of the recorded time and stop. At that point, we place a stake in the ground and tie a red flag—that will mark our medians."

"We plant the red flag and return here." Centori states, "Assuming we know what the hell we are doing. Based on the various distances between the mountains, Francisco will return first, I will be second and Justo last."

"Consider the time to our starting points, since that varies too," Griegos says.

"I said assuming we know what the hell we are doing," Centori admits his mistake.

After a good laugh, the three men mount up and ride in two directions: Centori and Griegos ride to the Sandias. At that point, they will split off to the Jemez and to the Otiz, respectively. Calabaza rides to the Ortiz and then to the Jemez.

Centori and Patriot take a slight lead in front of Griegos and his mount. At a steady pace, they ride to the foothills of the Sandia Mountains.

***

"Well Francisco, this is it," Centori says upon arriving at the Sandia foothills, "This plan just may work."

"If it doesn't, it is not for lack of trying!"

"Okay, let's mark time and go!"

"Adios! See you at the Circle C."

Centori and Patriot glide over the mesa. The lone rider heads to the Jemez Mountains. Within a few minutes of steady riding, a lone coyote appears and slowly crosses in front of horse and rider. Patriot reacts with a serious snort and stops in mid stride.

"Easy," Centori says as he leans forward and strokes Patriot's neck.

The solemn coyote remains planted in place and stares at Centori who uses the time to grab his canteen. He takes a quick drink, stares down the coyote and asks, "Are you here to question my decision again?"

No answer.

"So, you agree with my decision?"

No answer.

"I'll take that as an endorsement, Mr. Coyote."

Patriot fills the air with another serious snort; Centori pulls in the reins and moves around the coyote. An ear-piercing howl follows, causing Patriot to rear up and creating a dangerous moment until Centori's reassuring communication calms the horse down. They continue riding toward the Jemez.

Arriving at his destination, Centori enters San Felipe Pueblo and stops for some Indian frybread. Usually, he eats the flat dough fried in oil with honey, jam and beef. The fetish bear and the City of Gold will have to wait a few minutes as he eats the plain frybread. He checks his pocket watch, marks time and starts the return ride. He is careful to maintain the same pace, careful not to ride past the median.

***

Having travelled half the time of the first ride, he stops and says, "Well, Patriot, if this is not close to the median I don't know where it would be." He dismounts and drives the red stake deep into the ground. By late afternoon, Francisco Griegos rides into the Circle C and dismounts, exhausted from the long time in the saddle. Almost two hours later, with daylight fading, Adobe Centori returns equally fatigued. At dusk, the last tired rider appears. Justo Calabaza completes the mission and the angle alliance. All three riders planted red stakes and returned to the Circle C Ranch.

As the sun sets over the mesa, the men share their experiences over supper and a bottle of tequila. The three medians or midpoints of the mountain triangle are marked and prepared for the next phase of the search: finding the fetish bear.

CHAPTER 31

INTERSECTION

The following sunrise at the Circle C finds the same three men brought together by a series of events. It is another bright morning and another pot of coffee. They have a hearty breakfast and mentally prepare to find the centroid—and the fetish bear.

Centori pours another round and narrates, "We ride to the red stakes—the medians of the triangle—and wait. If we leave here at 10:00 am, we should be in position by high noon. Then, we ride from our positions, the medians, to the opposite vertex until we cross paths."

Griegos continues the recap, "Our compasses will show the general direction from the red stakes to the opposite vertex. Our intersection should place us at the centroid and near the bear."

"Yes, if we follow the imaginary line from our medians to the corresponding vertex, we should at least narrow the search to a reasonable area," Centori adds.

Calabaza continues, "At high noon we start at a slow gallop and fire a shot every 15 minutes and watch for our dust so we don't miss each other."

"Well, that is the plan," Centori says. The others laugh and Griegos adds, "Shall we go bear hunting?" Centori, Griegos and Calabaza mount up. They ride away from the Circle C in different directions and toward their assigned mediums.

CHAPTER 32

SWEET HEARTING

"We need more information," Carmencita repeats within the fragrance of strong coffee in the air.

The two attractive women, with tequila still in their heads, share coffee and a sunrise in the hotel room.

"Yes, you keep saying so," Sharon replies with emotionless eyes. "I must return to Gonzalo. I never stay away more than one day."

"When you are in bed with Gonzalo, talk about what you witnessed and heard. Determine as much as you can; I know you have your ways."

"Thank you, I think," Sharon says with a tone in her voice.

Carmencita smiles and responds, "We have no idea of the timing and there is no time to lose. You better act fast and find out what Centori and his partners have planned."

Sharon takes out a Marlboro Red Tip, lights her cigarette and says, "Take a breath, Carmencita."

"You say there are three in Centori's party?"

"I don't know, but I believe only those who came to my ranch are aware," Sharon affirms.

"*Your* ranch?" Carmencita quips.

Resenting the comment, Sharon adds, "Three men came to see Gonzalo is the point."

"We are only two, but I can even those odds and get the help we need."

"What are you talking about?"

"We need help in finding the mine and in extracting the gold ore. I have someone who will follow our orders without question."

"Because of your seductive beauty?"

"No, because it can be very unpleasant for him."

"What is his name?"

"Raphael."

"What happened to him?"

"It's not *what* happened to him—it is *what* happened to one of Mad Mady's soiled doves, Maise Maye. Raphael was involved with Maise's services upstairs at the saloon. At the end of their arrangement, they fought over the amount of payment. It became forceful and Maise got her gun and aimed. Raphael smashed a brass lamp against the wall. It ricocheted into Maise's head and killed her."

"What? Ricocheted?" Sharon widens her eyes in disbelief.

"Maise was never that lucky," Carmencita tries to conceal a laugh.

"So, why would he help you?"

"Because I saw him do it and could send him to prison."

"Why has he not killed you?"

"He is scared to come back to Mad Mady's Saloon."

"How the hell do you know that?"

"I know that and I can take care of myself. I am no Maise Maye," she boasts.

Sharon, inclined to agree with her, asks, "Was it an accident provoked by Maise, or was it a murder?"

"Maise ordered him out of the room, ready to fire in self-defense."

"So it was an accident?" Sharon questions.

"As the official record states, but I can swear it was murder."

"You didn't say so at the time."

"Correct."

"Why would you lie for him?"

"In case I needed him one day—you see! Besides, I never liked Maise very much."

"What exactly is your plan?"

"Allow them to lead us to the gold mine."

"It's not that simple."

"Simple enough. Find that location and take enough gold to finance my dream."

"What if they have the place guarded?"

"That is where Raphael comes into play."

"About last night, Senorita Carmencita, don't expect us to be sweet hearting."

CHAPTER 33

BEAR HUNTING

Adobe Centori continues to ride at a steady pace from his median. With Patriot's smooth gait, he makes progress toward his vertex; he senses that the other riders should appear soon. He fires off another shot from his Navy Colt as planned. There is no return fire. Stopping to retrieve his canteen, he rests his arm on the pommel on the saddle and waits in the silence.

Moments later, he hears a loud signal shot and urges Patriot forward. Ten minutes later, Francisco Griegos gallops in view of Centori who slows his pace. Griegos waves as he crosses Centori's path. Both riders turn around and meet.

Griegos offers, "Your fancy math plan worked!"

"At least this part. Let's see if Justo can find us. If not, we have our intersection that will help."

"All we can do is wait."

"Yep," Centori agrees while returning to his canteen.

The minutes pass with no gunshot sound to announce Calabaza.

"It may have been easier to find Pancho Villa than to find this damn bear," Centori says.

"From what I read, Pershing could say the same thing in reverse."

"Ha. Good point."

"Do you think Justo knows what he is talking about?"

"I know he believes in this chase___"

Bang. They hear a shot in the distance. Within minutes, Justo Calabaza arrives and crosses the others. He circles back to meet at the centroid of the mountain triangle, or what they perceive to be the centroid.

Centori yells, "Amazing, we did not miss each other."

The three horsemen unite. Any sense of victory is repressed by the absence of the fetish bear rock formation. They all wonder about the bear. Both Griegos and Calabaza look at the author of the math system application who responds, "Remember, from here we are on our own. We have narrowed down the search area; that is the best the math can do for us."

"Now, let's look for the fetish bear," Griegos encourages.

Calabaza agrees by saying, "Keep a sharp eye out."

Centori turns to Calabaza then scratches a pattern in the ground for the men to follow in their search. If anyone sees anything that looks like a bear, fire a shot. The other two ride to the sound. They take off in three different directions.

Adobe Centori continues to ride the range on his Circle C Ranch across the Galisteo Basin, out of sight of the others. Rider and stallion travel in a steady, forward motion. After hours of a seemingly endless hunt, the fetish bear, formed with rocks, remains unseen. Then in the near distance, an unusual shape commands his attention. He pushes Patriot forward as the rocky area comes into focus. Close enough. He dismounts and sees a pile of nondescript rocks with no sign of a mine entrance. In silence, a coyote boldly appears from behind the rocks and stares at Centori.

"You again!"

Centori swings back in the saddle. The coyote swings back into the den. Soon after, he sees another outcrop, pulls on the reins, stops and gets down. These rocks appear to mark an entrance to an old mineshaft. Yet, a closer examination reveals that a fetish bear shape is not in the rocks. Back into the saddle, he quickly reasons that centuries of erosion may have worn away any likeness to a fetish bear.

Sometimes in life, a split-second decision can have significant consequences. Centori dismounts again looks at the rocks and considers, *This could be the entrance indicated by the silver medallion... the entrance to the lost gold mine—the Seventh City of Cibola.*

Centori approaches what appears to be a barricaded entrance. He turns to look at Patriot who snorts his disapproval. It takes a few knocks of his Navy Colt for the old boards to fall away. He clears away debris from the opening and enters with extreme caution. Patriot snorts again. He ignores the warning, determined to go as far as the daylight permits.

Within twenty yards, he confronts a curve, defies his instincts and turns the rounded corner. Daylight is all but gone, but there is enough to see the sagging timbers. Shockwaves hit him at the sight of old timbers supporting the ceiling. He freezes and flashes on Gonzalo's warning, *Assume that any ramshackle support structure will collapse. The deeper you journey, the greater the danger. You could encounter cave-ins and drops at every turn.* Too late.

The ceiling trembles and threatens disaster. The quake puts Centori on high alert and raises his blood. His instinct is to turn and run. Could he outrun a collapse? A howl causes his head to turn. There it is—a natural niche in a wall. Intuitively, he moves into the niche, clear of the falling rocks and rubble loosened by the vibration—but it could be a death trap.

Seconds later, another howl encourages Centori to follow. Moving in the direction of the howl, he finds that the niche extends beyond its appearance. He feels open air then sees a coyote in a small opening. The coyote turns as if calling him forward. Coyote and Centori scramble from the mine through the small opening and into the adjacent coyote den. Daylight becomes immediately visible. They reach the surface as a thunderous sound of a cave-in fills the air. Patriot rears on his hind legs. The coyote howls again. Centori calms down Patriot and stares at the coyote and offers, "Thank you."

***

Around the same time, all three men realize that further searching would be useless. The men ride toward each other for some time and pull up. "Looks like the end of the trail," Centori shouts with defeat in his voice.

Griegos nods in agreement.

Turning to Calabaza, Centori offers, "I know this is a bitter disappointment. If anybody has a better idea, I'll listen."

Calabaza remains silent.

The three horses seem to ride in stride with each other.

CHAPTER 34

CROSSING THE BORDER

General Pershing's expeditionary army, organized into a division of three brigades, crossed the border into Mexico on March 15th without Adobe Centori. The general and 6,600 men marched in two columns from Columbus and Culberson's Ranch in search of Pancho Villa.

Units of the expedition include two infantry regiments, cavalry regiments, field artilleries, engineers, ambulance companies and a Signal Corps company. New Mexico National Guard units were stationed on the Mexican border. The troopers carry Springfield rifles and semi-automatic pistols.

Two days later, the 2nd Cavalry arrived at Colonia Dublan, where Pershing set up a command post. The 1st Aero Squadron with Curtiss Aeroplanes flew reconnaissance from Columbus. Then, the squadron flew to Pershing's command post. A few days later, Pershing sent the 7th Cavalry deeper into Mexico to start the pursuit. Then, the 10th Cavalry moved south by rail and the first Aero Squadron conducted aerial reconnaissance.

This was followed by the 11th Cavalry arriving in Columbus by train from Georgia and marching into Mexico. Additional aero squadrons were dispatched by the general to cover rough territory between the columns.

The expedition was hampered by bad weather, rendering the mission more challenging. There were 10,000 soldiers from the Regular Army and National Guard units dedicated to the expedition.

CHAPTER 35

TEA PARTY

No words are spoken on the ride back to the Circle C. Disappointment was in the air and in the dust. Centori is uncertain why Calabaza is returning to the ranch, but does not ask.

At the Circle C, the men stand under the portal and stare out onto the mesa. Two of them consider the adventure over and done. One does not.

"We have given a reasonable amount of time to the search," Centori says.

No reaction from Calabaza.

Griegos says, "More than reasonable."

"I don't see what more we can do," Centori goes on.

Finally, Calabaza asks, "What is reasonable with so much at stake?"

"We have no evidence," Centori replies.

"No one can find the bear unless shown."

"We have been shown. Don't forget the medallion." Centori shakes his head in frustration, "Justo, you are welcomed here at the Circle C anytime, but I am done chasing the bear."

Ignoring the statement, Calabaza calmly says, "Perhaps the Gila Wilderness can show us the way."

"How much more do you know? How much more does anyone know?" Centori exclaims.

Calabaza, who can read people, faces and movements, takes another approach by asking, "Have you been to the Gila Wilderness?"

Centori sighs and says, "Cliff dwellings, near the Gila River and Silver City."

Calabaza gives a firm nod and replies, "Yes, the Mogollon cliff dwelling ruins."

"TR established a national monument there a few years back," Centori says with fatigue in his voice.

"The Mogollon people inhabited caves and built connecting dwellings within the cliff. They used natural cover as a defense. Building homes into the cliff face and at high points provided much protection. If attacked they pulled up their ladders and ropes."

"Okay, I am sure you have a point!" Centori states.

"Try to see the homes from a distance—you cannot. They blend into the cliffs. Perhaps the fetish bear is hidden in the same way and can only be seen from the sky and___"

"Hold on." Centori interrupts and says, "Carlene and I covered the entire basin and saw nothing that looked like a bear!"

"Now that we know the centroid, an aerial search fixated on that area could reveal the bear."

"I find it extremely odd that we didn't see the bear from the air."

"Perhaps you were unable to recognize the bear."

Centori exhales heavily and repeats, "We thoroughly covered the basin."

"That was *before* we identified the centroid; we can focus on it with different angles."

"I worked through my doubts from the beginning and followed your direction. But now..."

"You have done so. I am thankful, but we have come too far to stop."

Griegos sees in the way Centori sets his jaw that Calabaza's argument is not persuasive.

"I have had enough and we do not have enough to continue. We have come to a conclusion."

Centori looks at Griegos for some kind of support. Instead, Griegos says, "It's a good excuse to see that good-looking pilot lady again."

Checkmate.

Centori could not hold back a big smile.

Reassured, Calabaza plays his last card, "There is something else," he says in a whisper.

Centori hurries him with his eyes.

"The limits of a closed mind are different from the limits of the world."

"Closed mind," Centori repeats, but not as a question.

"It is becoming clear to me that the fetish bear cannot be perceived with a closed mind. Only a free mind can see beyond the familiar world."

Both Centori and Griegos appear uncertain about Calabaza's meaning.

"I was wrong in the way we looked for the bear. I thought it would be clear to those who carefully searched."

"We were more than careful, Justo."

"Yes, we were but one last step appears to be needed. I am talking about peyote," he says in a voice of a sage.

"Unless you open your mind, it cannot be seen from the ground or the air," Calabaza states.

"Are you serious?" Centori asks sharply.

"For the sake of the pueblo people, trust me. The fetish bear is spiritual; peyote allows us to relate to the spiritual world."

Centori holds up his hand in rejection of the idea. Calabaza goes on, "We use a cup of tea—peyote tea. We use sacred peyote for religious ceremonies for a better connection to the spiritual world."

"I appreciate your customs but why do you say this now!"

"I was hoping not to say it at all. Now I see that it is needed."

"You are taking this too far."

Griegos remains silent and unsure of his opinion, but Calabaza continues, "The Silver Medallion and the fetish bear are mystical. Peyote cactus buds, brewed into a tea, will provide a new perspective into mystical parts of the world."

"Carlene is an experienced flyer and the plane ride was thorough—there were two of us looking for the bear without success."

"Two of us?"

"Yes, she knows. She was asking probing questions. I could not lie to her again. She is trustworthy."

"I don't know her."

"Well, I do!"

"Your view from the air was elevated, but your awareness was not elevated. The fetish bear fades to nothing without appropriate perception."

"You wish me to take peyote and fly above the basin?"

"Yes. The fetish bear will become clear."

"My vision is just fine, Justo!"

"Fine for the physical world, but not the spiritual world. You already have it inside you. The peyote will bring it out—and you will be able to feel and see beyond the physical world."

Centori thinks about General Pershing before Calabaza ends his sentence. Then he looks at Griegos for advice; he has none. They agree that Calabaza is manipulating, though not dishonest.

Calabaza presses, "Peyote penetrates the physical and allows us to see through things in the world: water, rocks, trees, plants and birds."

"Did you say birds?" Centori squints his eyes and reflects on the hawks that escorted the aeroplane.

"Yes, birds, if you are adjusted to hear their messages."

"I am more in tune with coyotes...a cup of tea you say?"

"Yes. First, I will drink a cup with you here, so you will know what to expect."

Centori turns to Griegos and offers, "Would you like to join a tea party?"

CHAPTER 36

SILVER WHAT?

"Are you sure?" Solana presses him. The morning sun shines over the splendid hacienda that represents Francisco Gonzalo's wealth. *Rancho de las Aquila* contributes much to the local economy and favors other landowners and businesses.

Gonzalo is generous to all who work on his ranch. He provides quality dwellings for the workers and a separate place for married workers. Yet, his generosity toward Solana is waning. Back at ranch, she makes the most of her naked breasts just inches away from him.

"Yes, I am sure. I can't tell you," he answers while leaving the bed to dress.

"You mean you won't tell me," Solana says sharply.

"Have it your way."

"Your secrecy is galling."

"I can say the same about you."

"Whatever do you mean?" she asks feigning calmness.

"I am not as foolish as you think."

Her resentment flares. She jumps up, presents her nakedness, and says, "You like what you see don't you?"

"You are cold and calculating, and I advise you to get dressed."

"Cold? I hardly think that is the case. You have not complained."

"Solana, I am growing weary of your antics. That was a very expensive vase!"

"You know I have ways to make you feel better."

He raises his eyebrows, sits down and pulls on his boots.

"We could leave here and tour Spain. Wouldn't that be wonderful?"

"I have a ranch to run."

"With enough money we could do anything."

"I have had enough. Why are you so interested in other people's business?"

"We both know the answer to that."

"Solana, you are wasting your time. Those men are wasting their time."

"You are confirming what I overheard?"

"Don't you mean spying on us?"

Still naked, Sharon smiles seductively.

"Get this out of your head. Those men are foolish. I have been in mining for most of my life. I know the Galisteo Basin; it is a waste of time."

"Yes, they seek a gold mine...just the three men who came here?"

"I suppose. What difference does it make?"

"No difference."

Gonzalo opens the door and reflects, "I thought Centori was smarter than that."

Sharon's face flares with rage at the sound of that name, "He is a damn fool!"

"Do you know him?"

"I have never been to the Circle C."

"That's not what I asked."

"No, I don't know him."

"Yet you know the name of his ranch."

"The Circle C is one of the biggest ranches in New Mexico."

"I see."

"Are you sure he is foolish?"

"Foolish enough to chase a Silver Medallion that has been buried for centuries."

"Silver what?"

CHAPTER 37

CLEAR ENOUGH

The evening dusk is closing in after a windy day. Downtown Albuquerque is quiet except for the Alvarado Hotel. Carlene Cortina rapidly agreed to Adobe Centori's dinner invitation. At half past six, they enter the same black oak paneled dining room. A Harvey Girl, who smiles her approval, escorts them to a table where they order drinks and settle into each other's sphere.

Her eyes are wide open; his eyes look directly at her and set on her alluring smile.

"Carlene."

"Yes, Adobe."

"I am happy you accepted my invitation."

"Honestly, I didn't expect to hear from you so soon. Do you need another flight?"

With lips slightly parted and before he can respond, she ventures, "I must admit, I was really surprised to receive an invitation."

"Pleasantly surprised, I hope."

"Yes, but my husband used to say there are no surprises. I never agreed with that."

"You are married? I didn't know!"

"You are not very attentive," she states while extending her left hand and ring finger.

"Where is your husband now?"

"He was killed two years ago in Vera Cruz."

That news stuns Centori, who refused General Pershing's request to re-join the army. He says softly, "I am sorry. Vera Cruz was the first U.S. intervention in the Mexican Revolution."

"I have been reading about General Pershing chasing Villa in Mexico."

"I know about that. Was your husband involved with the German ship carrying arms for Victoriano Huerta?"

"Yes. Wilson ordered the military to stop the shipment, causing a fight with Huerta's troops. My husband and other soldiers were killed. Huerta received his shipment when the ship docked at another port."

"I understand. I am sorry," he repeats before changing the subject with, "How did you become interested in flying?"

"As a young woman, I dreamed of soaring in the sky. I would stare upward for hours wondering about the excitement of flying. I dreamed of having wings and feeling the power of the air beneath me."

"That sounds wonderful and uplifting," he jokes inappropriately.

"Now I live the magic of flight, each curve, each angle. I love the far horizons and open space below. I never get tired of seeing the virgin wilderness of the sky. The beauty of the earth and of the heaven encircles me. Every time I fly in my aeroplane, I am ever so joyous, ever so free. Oh, I am going on and on."

"Please don't stop."

"Don't think you have to say that because of me."

"I want to say it because of you."

It is an affair of the moment until Centori says, "Would you be willing to conduct another air search of the basin? The same ground, but closer."

The charming effect that flows from her pretty voice ends, "And I thought this was a social event."

Crestfallen, Centori scrambles for recovery, "Yes, this is very social...I am happy to share a table with you."

"Are you sure?"

"What comes from the heart goes to the heart."

"That is very nice," she says.

"I can't take credit. English poet Samuel Taylor Coleridge said it first."

"Coming from you it sounds beautiful."

"You have a way with words, Miss Cortina! Are you willing to fly with me again?"

"Excuse me a moment."

"Of course," he says while jumping up.

She walks away. He studies her every step. She moves out of sight. He returns to his drink.

Soon after, she returns to the table and he offers, "Hello, Carlene."

"What? You saw me a minute ago."

"Yes, I know...but every time I see you it is like the first time."

"I see," she replies with suppressed surprise.

"Carlene, are you willing to fly with me again?"

She spreads her hands in a wide gesture, unsure of his intentions, but agrees, "Yes, I am willing."

"There is one more request; can we fly on a cloudy day? The sun was too strong last time."

"We flew on a clear sunny day. I do not understand. Most people prefer to fly on a clear day," she says and stares in a confused way. "Any other yarns you would like to spin?" she adds while folding her arms.

"I don't wish to bore you with cowboy business."

"You are not a cowboy; you are a ranch man."

He leans forward and drops his voice confidentially, "I suppose you should know."

She softens her cool blue eyes and smiles in agreement.

"Let's order dinner and I will reveal all to you," he promises.

"That sounds serious," she adds.

"What's serious, supper or the secret?" he jokes.

They share a shaky laugh.

She looks at him carefully, as if seeing something new in his demeanor. He reveals the true reason for his sudden interest in flying.

***

"I didn't mean to deceive you, Carlene."

"That's exactly what you meant to do, but you are not completely to blame."

"There are others involved."

"What a fascinating story," she says.

"You think it is just a story?"

She smiles and says, "I think it is important to you."

"You think Cibola does not exist?"

"It is called the legendary Indian City of Gold—legendary!"

"I understand how you feel."

"Not entirely. How about tomorrow afternoon. We can return to the sky."

"Yes, thank you."

"Remember, we fly low—we believe that the bear becomes visible in the afternoon shadows."

"Your reasoning is obscure in meaning, but as you wish."

"Thanks."

"You are most welcome. Let's meet at the airfield at 4 p.m."

"Okay, I will be there."

They finish their dinner, leave the hotel and walk to her Studebaker Speedster.

"Thank you for a lovely evening," she smiles.

He kisses her lips lightly and says, "Are my intentions clear enough?"

She is less shocked than she appears, "I will be ready to help find your bear."

He mounts Patriot and starts a happy ride back to the Circle C. She speeds away.

CHAPTER 38

MISSION CHURCH

Valtura, New Mexico

Raphael wears an old hat and a long coat which is a few sizes too big. Arrangements to meet behind the Mission Church on East Corona Street and Mission Road are in place. Carmencita stresses the importance of not attracting attention. The midnight hour suggests secrecy. They must evade any observation and avoid being overheard.

Raphael's unshaven face is blank, yet he glares at Carmencita. "You are late!"

Sharon, her expression stark, waits for an introduction.

His eyes narrow sharply, "Who is this?"

"You don't trust anyone," Carmencita barks.

"Why should I trust you?"

A barrage of strong words from her cause him to back down.

Her eyes flash in fury, and then she calmly says, "Meet Sharon."

Raphael looks at Sharon and returns his inspection of Carmencita, "You are most eager about this meeting, but why should I be?"

"I have an idea."

"I don't like it already," he states.

"*Espera un momento*. I have a job for you," she offers, "one that you will like."

"Don't be so sure of yourself," Raphael sneers.

"It is a profitable job that will be difficult for you to refuse."

"You think so? What kind of job?"

"We need you and your gun should we need protection."

"Protection from what?"

"My friend wishes to settle a score with one of Mad Mady's friends."

"Oh yeah, who?"

"It makes no never mind," Sharon chimes in.

"That's right. All you do is provide protection, if we need any. For your trouble, we will pay you five hundred; two hundred now and the rest when the job is done."

"What exactly is this job?"

"Watch the movements of Adobe Centori."

"Of the Circle C Ranch!"

"Yes."

Raphael barely controls his anger and spins halfway around before yelling, "Adobe Centori! Oh, I tell you women, you are crazy—the both of you!"

Carmencita explains, "You will not go anywhere near him, just tell us where he goes. Damn, it may already be too late. Think! You will no longer be tortured by the sight of me."

That remark, laced with her implicit power, eases his resistance. She notices the change in his demeanor and says, "Take this note. Read it and destroy it. I expect you will do well for us."

As Raphael withdraws with the note, Sharon softly says, "You never mentioned the murder of Maise Maye."

"I didn't have to," Carmencita says from rarefied air. "Now, what have you learned from Gonzalo?"

"They seek a kind of map showing the location of the gold mine. Without that map it is impossible to find the mine."

"Then we must wait for them to find that map."

"We could be waiting for a long time and Gonzalo thinks the mine does not exist."

Disappointed, Carmencita says, "We have no choice. We wait and hope that they find the map. In the meantime, at least we found each other."

"I told you don't expect us to be sweet hearting!"

CHAPTER 39

REVELATION PRELUDE

Barnstormer Carlene Cortina cancelled her aeroplane exhibition at the New Mexico State Fairgrounds in Albuquerque. The overcast day precludes a performance of her flying circus, but not the arranged flight with Adobe Centori.

Carlene, wearing the same dynamic flight outfit, leather headgear and jumpsuit, awaits Centori. At this time, he is camped on the mesa a few miles from Albuquerque brewing a cup of peyote tea.

Although the peyote is ready for drinking, he is reluctant and turns to Patriot. The stallion seems in favor of taking the tea. In uncertain times, he gives Patriot the benefit of the doubt. He takes the peyote tea and waits for the effects. Soon after, he proceeds to a meditative state, a nurturing of the spirit. He mounts up slowly and heads for Albuquerque.

***

"Adobe," she exclaims as he enters the hangar.

"Carlene," he replies with little enthusiasm.

"Are you okay?"

"Yes, good morning."

"You seem a little distant."

"Oh...not much sleep last night."

"Good morning to you too. It is a good cloudy day to fly," she quips. "The cloudy sky is as obscure in meaning as is the uncertainly of the search outcome."

Centori turns to an unknown man working on her aeroplane showing concern then turns back, "Thank you again, Carlene."

She hands over the headgear and goggles, and replies, "My pleasure."

Reaching into his shirt pocket, he informs, "This is a focused map of the center of the Circle C Ranch."

"I assume you wish to fly low again."

"As low as possible"

"I'll do my best," she smiles.

"You always do," he says while glancing at the unknown man.

This time she notices his concern and comments, "That is Werner, my mechanic. He is checking Jenny before we take off."

"That would be the better time to do so," Centori jokes nervously.

"Relax, this is a routine pre-fight check, and Werner is an excellent mechanic."

Werner pretends not to listen. He is a German citizen who recently returned from Berlin, which strengthened his ties to the Fatherland. The time spent in Germany has altered his point of view.

"With the basin area narrowed down on this map, we will have better luck," she says.

Centori's jaw sets because Werner is in listening distance. Yet, she continues, "We will descend as close to the ground as possible."

He does not respond, hoping to change the subject.

"*Alles gute Fraulein*," Werner says.

"*Danke, Werner*," Carlene replies.

Centori freezes at the sound of the German language and stares at her, "I didn't know you spoke German."

"*Nur ein wenig*, just a little. What is wrong?"

"Nothing," Centori answers while flashing on Jennifer Prower and her German saboteur organization—and their terrorist plots against New York. Although Jennifer is dead, German spying is not.

"You seem uneasy," she says while moving closer. "Do you have enemies?"

He moves closer to talk in a lower volume, "Every man does."

Puzzled by the comment, she offers, "I doubt you have foes."

"You would be surprised."

"Shall we find your fetish bear?"

They instinctively embrace, catching the attention of Werner. Then, he looks at Centori as if he knows something he would not reveal. In the cockpit, she starts the engine and waits for the takeoff signal; Werner removes the wheel blocks and waves. Then throttle up, acceleration and lift off.

The effects of the peyote tea and of Carlene's beauty are enough to drive him to distraction. After several minutes in the air and with the Circle C appearing in the distance, Centori regains focus. He must disconnect from a mental fixation of doubting the existence of the fetish bear. With that additional insight acquired from the tea, the fetish bear could appear.

Sailing in the air, Centori achieves additional awareness. The impenetrable riddle of the fetish bear suddenly seems less daunting. As they ascend, the sun hits the aeroplane with a flash of bright gold. She propels him through the sky. Peyote propels him through uncertainty of the bear's existence to exaltation.

The decisive moment is approaching, a moment to be convinced of the bear's reality. Up to this point, Centori was at an impasse, caught in thinking he had traveled through all the search attempts without success. If he disrupts his obsession on unsuccessful efforts, insight could emerge, allowing the bear to come into focus.

The engine noise and rush of air become still. Then, the wind resumes in an unusually, almost supernatural way as if to echo his whirling mind. The aeroplane seems to blend in with the sky.

From all the stimulus of the unnatural altitude that defies the laws of gravity, a mild trance emerges within him. He is motionless, adrift in a sky of indifference without scope. He floats above with sense of distance and direction gone—indifferent to the aeroplane and life hanging in the wind.

The increasingly crystalline clear air transmits brighter light, improves his vision, and allows him to see rock formations as never before. He looks up and down, then left and right, and stops. Two hawks appear on the right wing as if to guild him toward an epiphany. The birds close within a few feet, Centori takes notice. Birds-eye views converge in a downward manner as a prelude to revelation.

One second, two seconds, three seconds—while riveted below it hits like a strong wind. It all becomes clear—transformation complete. He looks straight into the heart of lightness where the fetish bear lies.

CHAPTER 40

EUREKA MOMENT

"Oh my God, there it is," Centori exclaims.

Pushing her shoulder, he screams over the sound of the engine, "Look, to the right. It is a bear in a rock formation."

She shakes her head, unable to see a bear in the rocks. He insists. She strains and yells, "I don't see anything."

Centori's sudden eagle-eyed insight escapes her. The bear remains unintelligible to her; she had not joined his tea party.

"Circle this area," he yells. "That is the legendary lost gold mine—the lost city of Cibola!"

"How can you be sure?" she yells and banks the plane.

He doesn't answer and notices the avian escort is gone.

"Lower," he yells.

She circles around and he begins to drop rocks painted red as markers around the fetish bear. Minutes later, he yells, "Let's go back!"

On the way back to the airfield, Centori feels the peyote effects waning, but not the excitement of finding the bear. He is riding on a cloud. On this less than sunny day they land at the airfield. She bounds out of the cockpit and brushes her hair out of her face. He jumps out and joins her; a warm embrace expresses their success. This time it goes on for quite some time. Overwhelmed by seeing the bear, he wants to touch her cheek, but he does not. He is powerless to explain adequately his amazement in seeing the bear. It does not matter; he feels peaceful by her closeness.

All things fade away: the Pershing affair, the trouble with Mad Mady, and even the discovery of the fetish bear. At this point, where his body meets his soul, Adobe Centori found the fetish bear within a spiritual world. At the same time, the revelation would become a salient story in his physical world.

"Thank you, Carlene. I will never forget your help."

"You are welcome. I have never seen you so excited! You finally found the bear."

"Yes, but my excitement has more to do with you than a bear."

A broad smile signals appreciation of the compliment, "Did you notice how close those birds were flying near us."

"How could I not notice?"

***

Centori, with the peyote effects gone, returns to the Circle C eager to share the news of the discovery of the bear. Galloping, he sees Griegos and shouts, "Francisco, we found it!" Coming to a quick stop, he dismounts, and goes on, "We found the bear. All became clear—it cried out to be seen from the air. We must go there first thing."

"Justo was right."

"Yes, and Carlene never looked so beautiful."

"Ha ha, good news—on both points," Griegos says.

CHAPTER 41

BARELY PASSABLE

The next morning in the Circle C kitchen, Centori and Griegos huddle around the table with predawn coffee, waiting for Justo who promised to return at sunrise. He does.

While pouring another cup, Centori says, "We know the general area of the centroid. We head there and start looking for the red markers I dropped around the fetish bear. We can examine the area to confirm it is an actual entrance to a mine."

"You still have doubts?" Calabaza asks.

"Let's finish our coffee and ride," Centori replies.

Lurking from a distance with a binocular in hand is Raphael, along with a newly hired man.

***

The three equestrians, with Centori in the middle, ride their horses in stride with each other. They move as a balanced force surging forward with a sense of purpose in the air. As they ride the range toward the elusive fetish bear—they ride into history.

About an hour later Centori shouts, "There they are! Just where I dropped them!"

Impulsively, he breaks into a gallop, leaving the others behind. Griegos and Calabaza break into a gallop and follow Centori to the red markers.

They dismount and circle the bear. High on a base of flat rocks there is a dramatic stone creature, striking in tranquility. In some way, the bear's features have resisted weathering. The eyes that watched the beautiful mesa and the perfect sky are sharp and proud. For centuries, the arched-back bear has seen seasons come and go; hawks have circled the bear and rattlesnakes have coiled in the shade of its base. Facing west, the bear commands respect for protecting an ancient place.

A deeply emotional Calabaza offers, "No matter what happens from here, I thank you—this is the ancient fetish bear, and his eyes seem welcoming. The pueblo elders and the spirits of our ancestors were right."

Standing at the fetish bear, Centori observes, "The mouth of the bear has a mound of rocks that could be covering up an entrance."

"Okay, let's put our backs into it," Griegos states.

Suddenly a strong wind rushes in causing the men to reach for their hats. The horses are startled and start to stir recklessly. Increasing wind speeds push the men down; they grab for any rocks and hold on helplessly. Then it stops.

Slowly, the men stand up and Centori says to Calabaza, "I thought you said the bear's eyes are welcoming."

"I'll check on the horses," Griegos says.

In the distance, Raphael's hat and binoculars blow away. His partner remains huddled against the surrounding rocks.

At the bear, they work to remove large rocks and small boulders that are around the bear's head and in the mouth.

Slowly and deliberately, they remove the obstacles to a point where a small space appears. They stop to assess and continue removing rocks, creating a larger space and exposing the open mouth of the bear.

"Wait, before we continue, let's confirm that this is a mine shaft opening; if not, we are finished with this treasure hunt," Centori asserts.

"I will explore."

"Are you sure about that? The opening is barely passable," Griegos jokes.

Centori pauses for a moment and replies, "Maybe we should remove some more rock."

Two minutes later, with enough clearance, they find a narrow passageway within the bears' head. Centori slips through an opening and drops down a short distance. The light above shines on the area. He walks a few yards.

"All okay?" Griegos calls down the opening.

"Yes, there is something here," he calls back then senses others in the space—it is a ghostly feel.

Strange images cause Centori to stop and stare. He feels an odd sense of anxiety that yields to relief. Standing in a somewhat inaccessible cave, he believes that the images are not living space decorations. Rather, the wall and ceiling paintings suggest a form of communication, without indication of past occupancy. The culturally significant images of animals and people are remarkable, especially the prominently painted fetish bear.

Within three minutes, Centori pops up from the opening like a prairie dog, bounds up and out of the bear's mouth and exclaims, "There is an old tunnel leading somewhere. I am sure that is true." Brushing himself off, he suggests, "I think we continue."

The others agree.

"Okay, good; the tunnel could lead to the mine. Let's protect this opening and cover it up until we are ready to proceed," Centori says while unaware of the prying eyes in the distance behind a rock formation.

CHAPTER 42

RED MARKER

Raphael's new hat is pulled down low as he enters Mad Mady's Saloon. Hoping not to be recognized, he stays alert while going upstairs and softly knocking on Carmencita's door. Having finished serving a client, she is half-undressed. He does not notice or he does not care. She notices and cares about a red marker that he drops at her feet.

"What the hell is that?" she demands while pulling on a robe.

"There are others like this one."

"Get to the point!"

They mark a spot in the basin. Centori and his friends seemed real interested."

"What spot?"

"I can show you where, but that's all."

"What kind of spot?" she demands again.

"It looks like a pile of rocks and some kind of hole in the ground, that's all I know."

"Show me now!"

"What's the hurry?"

"You fool! We must put the marker back before they find it is missing."

"It is a long ride," he insists.

"Let's go! We should be able to be there before sundown."

***

Carmencita and Raphael arrive at the site surrounded by red markers.

"What is this?" he asks.

"Why don't you climb down and find out?"

"No!"

"Do you remember where you picked up the red marker?"

"No."

"Of course not. Return it to where you think you picked it up."

Raphael looks at the other markers and drops his marker.

"Let's go. I need to contact Sharon."

CHAPTER 43

BATTLE OF PARRAL

Centori sits alone in his library. With the discovery of the fetish bear and a tunnel that could lead to the mine, he takes time to read an account of the recent Battle of Parral.

U.S. forces penetrated more than 500 miles south of the border to Parral in the Mexican state of Chihuahua. At that town, the U.S. cavalry engaged soldiers of Venusitiano Carranza. The Americans with an organized withdrawal repulsed the larger number of Carrancistas.

Although the U.S, cavalry was heavily outnumbered by the Carrancista solders, they repulsed the attack by withdrawing to defensive positions in Santa Cruz de Villegas. The Carrancistas are against Villa and the U.S.

Faced with a potential siege by the Carrancistas, the cavalry commander dispatched riders for obtain help. When Buffalo Soldiers of the 10th Cavalry entered Santa Cruz de Villegas, the Mexicans retreated to Parral, ending the battle. The Battle of Parral was a decisive time in the Mexican Expedition.

According to a newspaper report, General Pershing was "mad as hell." Now, he is fighting more than Pancho Villa's army, he must deal with a Carrancista army. Centori senses that the Battle of Parral is a turning point. The Carrancista's involvement could start a general withdrawal from Mexico.

CHAPTER 44

RECONNOITER

The next day, Carmencita, Sharon and Raphael ride to the area of the fetish bear. When they arrive, Raphael hides the horses and the women hide begin the rock formation. From that concealed distance, Carmencita and Sharon wait for Centori, Greigos and Calabaza to arrive at the gold mine entrance.

"Are you still dreaming about Los Angeles?" Sharon asks.

"Yes," Carmencita gleefully answers. "I hope to be in Downtown Los Angeles for the *Fiesta de Los Angeles* this spring. I received a postcard from a friend showing a parade that starts at the Old Plaza."

"Sounds wonderful," Sharon relies with sarcasm.

After securing the horses, Raphael joins the women.

"The parade ends in Fiesta Park where there are many event!" Carmencita adds.

"Wait," Sharon exclaims. "Listen, riders are approaching. Here they come!"

The women watch as three riders come into focus. Then, Centori, Greigos and Calabaza reach the fetish bear. Sharon watches for any reaction to the misplaced red markers. Perhaps dropped in the same place, perhaps not. The returning men appear not to notice any changes. The spectators who are reconnoitering from afar, notice all.

Pointing a long boney finger, Raphael says, "There is what you seek."

"There he is!" Sharon's face contorts at the sight of Centori.

Carmencita takes notice of the reaction and says, "Yes, there is what we seek—not who we seek."

"The great Adobe Centori," Sharon adds in an evil way. "Look, the other two men were with him at my ranch."

Carmencita rolls her eyes and says, "Your ranch. I see his friend Francisco. I don't know the third man."

"Who cares about the others?" Sharon asks.

Showing more concern, Carmencita reacts, "We will return when they are gone to see what's down there."

"Why wait?" Sharon asks.

The three men begin to remove the rocks covering the opening.

CHAPTER 45

FRENZIED FLIGHT

Three men stand at the centroid of the mountain triangle, at the fetish bear and at the mine entrance, armed with revolvers. Centori checks the needed equipment and turns to the other two men, "Are we ready for this?"

"Ready as I can be," Griegos answers.

Calabaza nods solemnly.

"Okay, let's find the legend," Centori adds and leads the way through the bear's head.

As the three men enter the fetish bear and disappear, Sharon expresses an all-consuming face of rage. Her excessive need for revenge is like a hungry wolf tearing apart rodents. The look on Sharon's face disturbs Carmencita. Raphael notices too and looks away.

Centori climbs down about ten feet and into a dark tunnel entrance. The others follow. With lanterns held high, they move slowly inward on a steep grade that gradually flattens to a slight grade. Airflow blows in from the opening as their eyes adjust to the fading light. Along the way, they admire the wall and ceiling images, especially when the lanterns emit a glittering circle of light on the walls. There is something mysterious about the light effect, something elusive, like a City of Gold.

After an easy walk of a few hundred feet, Centori stops and says, "So far there seems to be no danger of a cave in or bad air. There are no heaps of fallen rocks or rubble anywhere...so far."

Calabaza observes, "This mine was cut from solid rock. It should stand forever."

"Watch for any loose rocks anyway, especially if we encounter sagging timber supports or any weak structures that could collapse," Griegos warns.

While looking around, they nod in agreement and move on. Centori looks back over his shoulder; the entrance is no longer in view. Within another fifty feet, they hit level land and stop again. He turns to the others, "Remember the key dangers Gonzalo listed."

Griegos says, "Watch for water drainage and ventilation, open shafts and holes that could contain water."

Calabaza follows with, "Beware of abandoned equipment, it could be explosives, chemicals or wire—I doubt we will find anything like that in this ancient mine."

"Right, but watch out for rattlesnakes, they are timeless," Centori grimaces.

"Rattlesnakes like open rocky places that provide protection, prey and basking areas," Calabaza adds.

"We did not see any around the bear's head where there is light. We should be clear," Griegos agrees.

"Watch out just the same! There is always a calculated risk, an unexpected factor," Centori cautions.

"Justo, remember to mark our path."

"Yes, I will make arrows with small rocks, marking the way and scratch the cave floor as we move on."

"Good. Francisco, note any landmarks and I will constantly survey our surroundings and mark all intersections," Centori says.

As they gradually move into the unknown, shadowy tunnel, the strangely quiet mine causes concern. It is so quiet that a soft sound hits the men's ears. They stop as if expecting something to happen. They are right.

Within fifty or sixty feet, hundreds of dim eyes confront them. The men freeze and cannot make out shapes. Then a massive wave of airborne creatures move in frenzied flight toward the men. Their nostrils fill with a strange scent. In a flash, wind and wild noises surround the men. Instinctively, they cover their heads. Deafening squeals and screams fill the cave with fear. Beating wings fly over and around the men. As suddenly as it started, it is over.

A large colony of disturbed bats exhibited uncanny skill in avoiding the men. The bats disappeared in seconds, having expressed displeasure with the intruders.

"That is something I will not soon forget," Centori says with a stressed voice before taking a deep breath.

The others nod, too stunned to voice a reaction. For the next few minutes, they move along a narrow path, their clothes dustier than before.

Centori, in the lead, comes to a split tunnel and asks, "Which way?"

Heavy sighs provide no answer.

"One tunnel is as good as the other," he says. "How about tossing the medallion?"

Calabaza, stares at Centori, then agrees, "Heads for the right tunnel and tails for left tunnel." He clears away a patch of dirt, smooths the area of rubble and tosses the medallion.

"Heads it is," Centori calls out.

Calabaza places a marker down and they take the tunnel on the right. Soon after, they turn sideways for a several yards in order to pass through an even tighter passageway. Deeper and deeper they explore remote parts of the mine, seeking any indication of the mother lode or at least a gold vein.

In the lead, Centori suddenly feels faint, staggers and falls forward.

"What is it, Boss?"

"Bad air, turn back," he gasps.

CHAPTER 46

UNFINISHED BUSINESS

"We have seen enough. Let's go back to Valtura," Carmencita repeats.

"That's not exactly how I see things. There is some unfinished business concerning Centori," Sharon replies.

"I knew it!"

"We agreed to get enough gold for my purpose, nothing more."

"Gold?" Raphael repeats with a surprised look.

"Now you have done it," Sharon mocks.

Turning to him, Carmencita explains, "We are not sure what's down there."

"You were sure enough not to tell me about the gold!" he replies.

"Stop it!" Sharon yells out.

Raphael, down with gold fever, stares at Carmencita who says, "Remember our plan, Sharon."

CHAPTER 47

WHITE STONE

Griegos and Calabaza rush to Centori and feel an airless wave oncoming. They grab him and retreat quickly.

"Are you okay?" Griegos asks.

Taking a moment to recover, Centori replies, "I will be. Let's hope the gold mine is not in that direction."

"If it is here at all," Griegos states to the disappointment of Calabaza.

"We should return to the tunnel split point and try the left tunnel," Calabaza responds quickly.

They return to the marker and take the tunnel on the left. Moving along with caution, they scan the walls. Then Centori suddenly trips on loose rocks near an open shaft, "That was damn close." He exhales hard.

They walk in silence through unclear geology with some progress. Soon after, they encounter a vertical mineshaft that was backfilled and capped with rocks.

"This is a dead end. Wherever this passageway leads to is beyond reach," Griegos says.

"Maybe it was for ventilation," Centori suggests.

A short distance away, Calabaza sees a sloping shaft and says, "Look over there. We have no choice." He places markers points and leads the way along the tracks.

Moving carefully, under the dipping silence of the earth's unsettling interior, they come to the end of the shaft that stops at a mound of rocks.

"This is another dead end," Griegos says, "We are at an impasse, do we stop?"

"Guess the Silver Medallion was wrong," Centori lets out.

"This is an indication to seek another way," Calabaza says with authority.

"I am not so sure," Centori says. "We haven't missed any other passageways. Hope your other way is better in predicting the gold mine location."

"We can turn around and head for the entrance. If we get there without finding anything else, we end the search," Calabaza proposes.

"Sounds reasonable," Centori replies as Griegos nods his head in agreement.

They retrace their steps, turn a corner, discover a narrow crawl space in a wall, and stop to stare.

"It is barely wide enough for a man to enter and barely visible," Centori observes.

"How did we miss this coming in?" Griegos asks.

"We were not looking for it," Calabaza replies. "There was no question of secret passages or secret rooms."

"Justo, this was your idea. Be my guest," Centori says.

"Yes, we are here because of me. I should be the one."

"No, this is the Circle C. Give me a boost up."

Moving around a rock pile and toward the wall, they raise him up. He turns and grips the crawl space edges. Once in the opening the others place a lantern behind him. All feel the tension of the moment, especially Centori who enters an unknown place and crawls slowly by the dim light. As he advances, time slows and the space becomes more unnerving. His heart pounds. He steels himself against an increasing sense of danger and keeps moving. There is nothing Griegos and Calabaza can do except wait.

Within twenty feet, Centori hits the end of the conduit and feels an immediate sensation of dread. A barrier prevents further progress. He strikes a match; it sounds mysteriously loud in a place draped in a heavy stillness. Waving the match slowly, with an increased pulse rate, he thinks, *What am I to do now? Oh what fools these mortals be.* He leans into the barrier. It does not move, no matter how hard he tries. "You okay?" Griegos yells.

No response.

Centori notices an out-of-place white stone in the upper right corner and considers the situation, *What the hell! I could be riding the range with Patriot, flying in the sky with Carlene or riding with Pershing but here I am.* Focused on the white stone, his lips tighten and his shirt becomes damp with sweat.

Griegos yells out again.

"Yes, okay at the moment," he yells back and thinks, *What happens if I yank the stone out?*

The prolonged silence is interminable. Then they all hear it—a sound of crashing rocks. The other men are jolted.

"Boss!" Griegos screams.

No answer. Breaking through the deafening silence, he screams again, "Boss!"

CHAPTER 48

GOLD FEVER

Raphael's scrutiny of Carmencita continues. She shakes off his stare and says, "When they are gone, we get the gold ore and haul away as much as possible. If there is anything at all," she says returning Raphael's stare. "Then we go to the assay office in Albuquerque."

"No," Sharon retorts.

"Your purpose is more than getting gold. You want revenge on Centori—you can do it alone!" Carmencita declares. "Remember our plan!"

"I remember that Centori sent me to prison and he broke my sister's heart!"

"Prison?"

"Oh Carmencita, you say it like you are an innocent flower."

"Why were you in prison," Carmencita demands.

"It was a little misunderstanding. I was released for good behavior—but you don't understand."

"All too well! You intend to settle the score with Centori."

"My intentions are more practical."

"Sure, Sharon—I told you when they leave we get the gold ore."

"Once inside, where would you look? How would we begin? We need them to show us the way, to show us exactly where the gold ore is located."

"I'm not sure about that."

"I doubt you have any mining experience. Are you willing to wander around a dangerous, dark mine not knowing where the gold is located?" Sharon says.

"She is right. We may not be able to find the gold without following them," Raphael says.

"I know gold when I see it!" Carmencita retorts.

"Do you? Are you sure you know what to look for?"

Carmencita comes around enough to ask, "What is you plan, Sharon?"

CHAPTER 49

POINT OF NO RETURN

Centori hauls himself back to the others, drops down and declares, "It's another passageway."

"What happened? What was that crash?" Griegos asks anxiously.

"A wall of rocks ended the crawl space. It seems man-made and it could be unstable. I removed a keystone and the wall fell inward revealing another space."

"There is always a calculated risk, an unexpected factor," Griegos repeats.

With dark humor in his voice he says, "Yeah, can't say I have been in a tighter spot. The crawl space opens to a small tunnel that seems to lead to a larger tunnel, probably not used in years."

"Or centuries," Calabaza says with satisfaction.

Centori declares, "We need to have a point of no return. If anyone feels that we have gone too far already, say so."

The decision is unanimous. They will continue.

They light matches and pass through the crawl space. Once through the rough, confining space, they drop down and enter the small tunnel. After the dark descent, they reach into the equipment bags and light torches. The flames improve the illumination and cast shadows as they explore the tunnel with a possible larger space beyond. The tunnel is high enough for the men to stand and walk without restrictions. Relief from the nerve-rattling experience is short-lived but welcomed. Every subterranean step on the dry and dusty ground could place them closer to danger and death. As they follow a one-way secret path, the air becomes hot.

"We are getting close to what I saw from the crawl space," Centori points out.

They approach what could be an entry to the larger tunnel. Then, in the near distance, an archway comes into focus.

"It didn't look that way from afar," Griegos says.

"It is obstructing a much larger tunnel beyond," Calabaza contends while touching the cold structure blocking an apparent entrance.

"We don't know that for sure," Centori replies. "There could be many additional caves, some natural and some artificial. A labyrinth of linking tunnels."

"We must find out."

"There is a series of tunnels and caves inside this mine, which is clear."

Calabaza goes on, "We did not expect this."

Centori responds, "There must be a ton of earth here. The rocks appear to have fallen perhaps due to an ancient landslide."

"We have to unblock this old tunnel," Calabaza says.

"Do we?" Centori asks dispassionately. "We have descended deeper than anticipated. We are beginning to worry, I'm sure."

Calabaza implores, "Think of possible gold in complete darkness yards away."

"Possible gold. We do not know the extent of the labyrinth in this mine. We could be wandering around for hours. Okay, break out the trench shovels," Centori says, "If we find another closed-off passageway, that will be the end for me."

After carefully removing rubble and creating a window-sized hole, Centori extends the torch forward, providing a dim view of the void beyond and of the danger. They work and expand the hole large enough for them to step through the blockage and rubble. The men stare into the cathedral-like chamber of caves that had not seen human visitors for centuries, so expansive that it renders them speechless. Then, they crash through the opening and enter the cavern.

"These hidden passages and caverns are amazing," one of the men finally says.

"Look at that designed archway with a block formation supporting it—not a common architectural site in a mine—and beautifully integrated with the stalactites," Centori adds.

"Yet, no gold," Calabaza states. "The chamber could be part of a network of tunnels yet to be found."

"Where do we go from here?" Centori says while viewing several complex passages. Then, he sees a faded image of a heavily carved door. "This way!"

They walk a short distance then stop in amazement.

"It's more than twenty feet high and ten feet wide...look at that ornate stone carving," Griegos exclaims.

"This is definitely man-made," Centori jokes.

CHAPTER 50

QUEEN OF THE DOVES

Sharon, Carmencita and Raphael continue to wait from afar as Centori, Griegos and Calabaza continue their subterranean mission.

"My plan is better. Centori will show us the way to the gold," Sharon declares.

"Of course, he will gladly tip his big hat and escort us to the gold. You are starting to worry me," Carmencita says.

"So you think we can navigate the mine and find the gold on our own?"

No answer.

"As I expected. Centori will create the path that we need."

"And he will wave us on!" Carmencita says.

Sharon snarls and replies. "No, we will follow the tracks from a safe distance."

"What do you mean? Are you saying we go into that hole in the ground?"

"Do you want your fancy life in Los Angeles or not?" Sharon tests.

Carmencita's eyes widen as she declares, "We must go back to Valtura as we agreed and return when it is safe. We can find the gold after they are gone."

"Are you willing to take that risk? We know nothing about mining. Perhaps you like being queen of the doves at Mad Mady's Saloon."

"Mad Mady does not call me that!"

"That's *Miss Mady* to you and the rest of your flock of doves," Sharon replies. Carmencita asks, "What do you know about tracking anyway?"

Raphael offers, "Looks like the mine has been closed for a long while, so following fresh tracks should work—provided I get an equal share of the gold."

No answer. Instead, Carmencita flashes a warning from her fiery eyes.

CHAPTER 51

LEGEND

All three men gather at the door to receive the full impact. The discovery places a mystified look on their faces. Calabaza feels the woodcarving and says, "It was probably made by ancient Puebloans."

The crude image shows humans as stick figures and a curve with rays springing forward. Excitement about what could be beyond this barrier fuels their next move. Calabaza gently tries to open the door—a door that has remained closed for centuries will not yield easily.

"It looks too heavy to take a shoulder to it," Griegos says.

"And too important to destroy," Calabaza says.

"If we can force it open a little to see inside..." Centori adds.

"Wait. The door may be unlocked. It may seem odd, but the hidden passages provided the needed security," Calabaza opines.

"Be my guest," Centori says.

Calabaza pushes hard with both hands, leaning his back into the effort. Nothing.

"It's frozen in place," Griegos figures.

He tries again and to everyone's surprise, the door creaks and concedes enough for Calabaza to reach in with his light—he catches sight of a scarcely perceptible huge chamber.

"What do you see?" Centori calls out.

"Wonderful things!"

With much effort, Centori and Griegos push the door open wide. They step inside of the chamber and scan the walls and ceiling of the geological beauty. Then a spectacular array of light gleams reflectively from their flames. They raise the torches for a better view and see a magnificent prime vein of gold ore.

"*Santa María madre de Dios,*" Griegos whispers in an awed voice.

CHAPTER 52

SERPENTINE SMILE

Sharon leads the way to the fetish bear. From a distance of 50 feet from the mine entrance, she whispers, "Stay here with the horses."

A nervous Carmencita protests, "I am not sure about this play."

"I thought you were afraid of nothing," Sharon replies with a serpentine smile.

"This does not make sense! We can find the gold on our own."

Raphael interjects, "This is our chance. You don't have to come into the mine. Just hold the horses for us. When we come up, we ride out fast. Be ready for us!"

"That's right. We will go down, see where the gold vein is located and quickly return," Sharon says in support.

Carmencita, with much trepidation, asks, "What if they see you?"

"Let me worry about that, *queenie!*" Sharon replies. "Think of the refined life and real respect that awaits you in Los Angeles."

"We are in this together."

"Look, we will follow them until they show us the gold. Then quickly leave the mine. Once we return, we all mount up and get the hell out of here."

"You thought of everything."

"I always do."

"Except if they see you, we can't return for the gold! Not to mention Centori would pursue us as claim jumpers."

"If they are chasing us, we fire a few shots to scatter their horses. All you have to do is stay here and wait for us."

Raphael drops down the fetish bear entrance. He looks up and tries to help Sharon down. She slaps away his help.

CHAPTER 53

HIDDEN CITY

"*Veta madre*," Calabaza exclaims. "There it is—the main gold ore vein!"

A majestic cavern of astounding stalactites and stalagmites stuns the men. There are incredible formations, fantastic pillars and color—especially the gold vein that sparkles despite the dim lighting. All around there are elaborate natural decorations—none more striking than the gold vein.

The chamber appears to measure about 1,000 feet by 750 feet with a dramatic ceiling about 300 feet high. It is not a city of gold. It is a wondrous natural environment with amazing natural beauty.

"Still don't believe in legends, Mr. Centori?" Calabaza says in a cavern with fabulous acoustics. "Look at the shine!"

Centori stands in stony silence before saying, "Congratulations, Justo. You were right. This is the stuff dreams are made of, especially if you were a Spanish conquistador."

"You may become a legend now," Calabaza proclaims.

"As long as I am a living legend; too many close calls," Centori replies.

"Yes, and you stayed true and on course, despite your doubts."

"You tolerated my doubts."

"Yes," Calabaza smiles. "This discovery means many good things for the pueblo people."

"This is not a hidden city, but the cavern was hidden all right!" Griegos observes.

"Yes, all that glitters here *is* gold!" Centori replies. "Let's take a gold ore sample for analysis."

They break out small tools and start chipping away.

With a small amount of gold ore packed, Centori says, "Now let's retrace our steps and go home. Hope our breadcrumbs will return us to the bear."

CHAPTER 54

MATTER OVER MINE

In the shadows, about fifty feet away, Sharon draws and cocks a small caliber revolver.

"What the hell are you doing? Let's get out of here," Raphael whispers.

"Too late. They will see us."

"Damn you."

"Shut up or I will cut you off—and I don't mean in mid-sentence. Now shut up. They are close—get ready."

When Centori sees the daylight stream in from the entrance, he turns to Griegos and Calabaza and announces, "Good job with the markers."

As soon as Centori finishes the sentence, a gunshot rings out. Sharon has no reservation about killing her target, but misses.

Gunfire erupts making the mine more dangerous. Bullets shatter a hard rock wall and miss the target. Instinctively, Centori dives down as rock shrapnel falls on his head. Calabaza drops down to one knee, draws, and waits for a target. Griegos stumbles to the ground, pistol in hand, ready to shoot on sight.

In the next instant, Centori scrambles to his feet, hugs the wall for cover and reaches for his Navy Colt—it is gone. An empty gun belt remains. Jolted loose by the fall, the gun is a few feet away. With gritted teeth, he rolls over and grabs his Navy Colt, swings the barrel and shoots from a prone position.

Seconds later, a shadowy figure levels a gun and resumes shooting. Centori sees the gun pointed and dives down again. Griegos and Calabaza join the gunfight with a hail of bullets. Powerful forces push Raphael back; his pistol flies from his hand. He leans forward, falls backward and is dead before hitting the ground.

A lone shooter fires back despite the odds. Rapid firing, bullets fly, passing each other in blinding flight. Sharon's rage gushes out in waves of fury in the face of heavy fire. An insane scream—fueled by sheer rage—echoes from her to the corners of the mine.

Sharon fires again, incoming bullet hits a wall behind her. The bats return and react to the chaos and horde around her. She covers her head and violently waves her arms—frantically fighting off the furious bats. Forced to retreat, she backs into a pitch-black space and stumbles. Then, she fills the chamber with a blood-curdling scream that reverberates like a grand crescendo. Then silence.

Carmencita retreats rapidly from the bear's head and mounts her horse. She rides out, hell bent for leather. The ambushed men wait a moment before slowly inspecting the underground battlefield.

Centori approaches a fallen figure with caution, his Navy Colt at the ready. Raphael's blank emotionless eyes are staring up. Closer now, his dead eyes are no longer a threat. They cautiously continue, expecting to find more bodies. They do not.

Sharon was quite insane. Now, she is quite dead. When the bats attacked, Sharon fell down a shaft—an almost bottomless pit. Then, she arrived in Hell where screams are louder.

Lack of resolve, not virtue, caused her failure. Vengeance mattered more than the gold mine. This time it is for real: Santa Fe Sharon is no more.

"Everyone okay?" Centori shouts.

The others call out and then join him around the body.

Griegos says, "What the hell was that?"

"Good old fashion claim jumpers, I guess," Centori says. You recognize this guy?"

"Never saw him before," Griegos answers.

Calabaza shakes his head from side to side, then moves to the open shaft, looks down into the darkness and says, "It sounded like the screams of a woman."

"It sure did," Centori agrees.

One day, they may learn what happened to Santa Fe Sharon.

CHAPTER 55

INTERLUDE

Centori hired Francisco Gonzalo who provided the expertise, equipment and miners to work the gold mine. His team of professional miners extracted an estimated one million dollars of the precious metal from the fetish bear mine.

Some weeks later, with the excitement over the gold discovery decreasing, Centori seeks another type of excitement. Carlene Cortina agreed to meet him in the Alvarado Hotel. The dining room is alive with conversation and the clatter of tableware. She observes him over the rim of her glass, takes a sip of wine and ventures, "Let me guess, you seek another aeroplane ride!"

"Carlene, my interest in flying with you goes beyond my ranch work."

"Yes, I know. You gave up that pretense."

"Yes, I did. I never met anyone like you."

She turns her smile on in a dramatic way and says, "I could say the same for you."

"The way you handle that aeroplane is miraculous. You are a great driver in the Studebaker Speedster too."

"I was showing off for you," she says with a smile.

"It worked."

He thought about reaching across the tabletop to take her hand. Instead, he reaches for his wine glass.

"I have been thinking about how close those birds were to my aeroplane."

"It was curious," he says.

"Dangerous too," she reacts. "Those birds could have been killed by my propeller."

"Has that ever happened?"

"Not to me. Anyway, that would be an accident, but the killing of birds today is on purpose and pervasive—mostly for ladies' fashion. Did you notice women's hats as we walked to our table?"

"How could I possible notice other women when I am with you?"

"Ha, but you can when you are not with me."

They both laugh and she goes on, "So many feathers adorning their hats as fashion decorations!"

"Some hats have a complete stuffed bird," he adds.

"I thought you didn't notice other women when you are with me," she teases.

"It was just the birds, not the women."

"Sure, Adobe."

"Anyway, it is not just fashion that hurts birds. Some birds suffer from overhunting as a cheap source of food. Sadly, the passenger pigeon became extinct a few years ago from overhunting and deforestation that destroyed their habitat."

"Passenger pigeon—that is an interesting name," she says.

"The name is from the French word, *passenger*, which means passing by in reference to their migratory ways."

"You know much about pigeons."

"Not so much, Carlene."

"Well, you indeed made much news with your gold discovery."

"There were others involved and none more so than you."

"I just gave you a ride."

"We were flying into history, and once all gold ore extraction and accounting is done, I will show my appreciation."

"That is not necessary. Do you believe that the fetish bear is enchanted?"

"New Mexico is a strange land of enchantment and mysteries. Some say this land attracts magic from the stars and from across the centuries."

"That sounds lovely," she chimes.

"In the everlasting extents of the high-desert, only rocks endure the passing of time. Rocks contain the land's history and as Justo has shown us—its secrets."

"Certainly, no rock in New Mexico ever had a more significant secret than the fetish bear," she states.

"I appreciate your sentiment, Carlene, and will show my appreciation."

"I said that is not necessary, Adobe."

"I would love to do so—I know how to say thanks!" he smiles broadly.

"Love, you say! There is gossip that says you were in love one time in your life."

His smile disappears.

"I do not abide by the idea that there is only one true love," she offers while raising her glass.

"I see."

"Can it be true that no other woman can compare to her?" she inquires.

"It is not true."

Enjoying her victory, she adds, "It may be sweet, but one true love is highly impractical."

"I take your point."

***

After dinner, they walk outside a short distance and sit on a bench near a big cottonwood tree on First Street. Downtown Albuquerque is quiet under a full moon that is brilliant in the cloudless night. The moonlight streams through the branches and shines on them. She feels happy; he is the reason for her state of mind. Although she planned to keep some distance from him, she moves closer, expecting a kiss. She is disappointed.

Two small birds fly overhead and perch on the cottonwood tree causing a stir in the branches. She looks above and says, "We seem to attract birds."

"You seem to attract me," he endeavors.

"You have been thinking about this moment."

"Yes, I have."

"Attraction is not enough," she says.

"It started from the first time we were in the sky together."

As open as a woman can be, she looks into his perfect blue eyes and asks, "Will you fall in love again and stay in love?"

Carlene's irresistible beauty moves him to kiss her full lips. It takes a few moments before her breathing slows down. *I have a room in this hotel, Room 104 in case you are interested,* she thought and then asks, "Do you dream about love?" pressing an earlier point. "If not, then loneliness. The kind of solitude that howls through the night like a plaintive wail of a coyote."

They remain quiet and watch the two birds above. Never in her wildest dreams had she thought of being so aggressive. It would be sensible to end the evening. Yet, it takes a few moments for her to whisper, "Tomorrow, I have a show at the airfield. I am staying overnight in the hotel, room 104."

Carlene embraces her passion. Especially for a woman who has been without passion for too long. It takes less time for him to agree. Under different conditions, she would have expressed the composure she has known throughout her life. She stands, holds her head high and walks back into the hotel. In a stately manner, she strides through the lobby as though she is the Queen of England and the people are British subjects.

***

Immediately upon entering her room, Centori admires her small waist, slender body and released hair. She kicks off her shoes, rolls down her stockings and skillfully removes her dress and undergarment, revealing herself.

"You are more beautiful than I envisioned," he offers.

In an excited pitch, she says, "Thank you for noticing. I did not anticipate the impact of your company."

"I did not anticipate the openness of your response," he adds.

He removes his shirt and conducts a sweeping embrace, fitting into the shape of her body. She follows with a stronger embrace, arches her body against his body and exhales.

Tumbling into bed, he lightly runs his hands over her body. Carlene shuts her eyes and allows him to continue. He answers by gently caressing the most intimate part of her body. She raises her arms wide over her head, signaling and allowing him to continue.

At times during their lovemaking, she moves slowly, her resistance becomes neutral, as if the last time. Embracing her shaking body, he gently rocks her in his arms. Her moans of pleasure yield to a song of rapture.

***

The stars begin to fade from the sky as Carlene smiles at him and says, "I have taken you for a ride of a lifetime in the heavens. Now, you have returned the favor!"

CHAPTER 56

CHIMAJA WHISKEY

It is Sunday, but today the Sabbath calm stops at the Circle C Ranch. Centori is hosting a party to celebrate the finding of the so-called Seventh City of Gold. On *La Placita* the guitars, trumpets, violins and harp of the Mariachi are far from tranquil, exciting the crowd with simple and subtly complex rhythms on this memorable day. The musical group is dressed in silver-studded charro suits and ornately stitched Mexican sombreros.

Pueblo leaders and their families, ranch hands, select people from Valtura, University of New Mexico archeologists and newspaper reporters are watching women dancers in flouncy dresses. The Mariachis are the soul of Old Mexico and of New Mexico, and the singular sound of a fiesta. Standing close to the jubilant and vibrant women dancers is Mad Mady who has pulled back emotionally from Centori, but remains a loyal friend.

As a native New Yorker, Centori sometimes misses the cooking aromas of his youth. Gefilte fish of his Jewish neighbors, corned beef stew of his Irish neighbors and spaghetti sauce of his Italian family are a far distance from New Mexico. Today, *Carne asada* is marinating with lemon, lime and pepper on a large grill.

While the party goes on outside, Centori, Griegos and Calabaza meet inside. Assembled in the library, the men review relevant documents created by Albuquerque lawyers. Centori gives 50% of his share to Griegos. In addition, he gives 10% divided among a list of several people. Beneficiaries and amounts of money appear in the papers:

- National Autonomous University of Mexico, in the name of Gabriela Zena
- Elizabeth Blaylock, Valtura, New Mexico
- John Murphy, Washington City
- Rocco Grandinetto and Jack Haughey, NYPD
- Parents of Charity Clarkson, Weston, Connecticut
- Circle C Ranch Cowboys

"A large share of the gold mine is for the pueblo communities as agreed and indicated in these papers," Centori says to Calabaza. "Most of the gold goes to the pueblo people. I hope you agreed that the percentages reflect our agreement."

"Yes, that is generous, more than our agreement! Thank you for believing in my story."

"Ha, thanks for tolerating my doubts."

Griegos and Calabaza laugh aloud. Centori adds, "It was a long road with much anticipation, but all worthwhile."

Calabaza says, "Mr. Centori, I have a special request."

"Yes, what would that be?"

"I would like you to have the Silver Medallion."

"That is a great relic of your people!" Centori exclaims.

"You have greatness of the soul. It is appropriate to accept the medallion. Honor our people, honor me."

Griegos nods his approval and Centori responds, "Thank you, Justo, thank you very much." He takes the leather wrapped medallion, places it in the top draw of his desk and declares, "Now, how about joining the party?"

All move toward the door, then Centori asks Griegos, "Oh, one more thing, Francisco, please ask Mady to come in for moment."

If Mady had any reaction to Sharon's claim about intimacy with Centori, she hid it well. Sharon was a known serial liar and he would not be seduced, she kept telling herself.

"That is quite the party, Adobe," Mady says as she walks into the library.

"Mady, sit down."

"Okay, sounds serious."

"I have bank drafts for you," he says with a kind smile.

"Oh."

He hands her an envelope. Mady's eye widen at the amounts. "Adobe..."

"Please accept one draft and distribute the other to any family of Berta Brandt."

"Berta?"

"Yes. I always liked her. She was an innocent victim of your saloon take-over plot."

"Berta has a sister named Opal who lives in Texas. I can track her down. You are the most generous man in Valtura, probably in all of New Mexico," Mady exclaims.

Centori, who referenced Sharon by mentioning Berta's murder, asks, "Mady, are we ever going to talk about your sister?"

"Not today."

"Okay. Let's join the party."

"Let's do so."

Perhaps Gabriela's ghost comes between them; perhaps Mady is not dangerous enough. In any case, Centori's relationship with

Mady has reverted to a previous time. It was quite natural to return to friendship after leaving his romantic sphere.

Returning to *La Placita*, Centori and Mady join Griegos, Calabaza, Quesada, and Conrado at the head table. Suddenly, a distant rumble captures the attention of some of the guests. Then, a loud rumble causes all of the guests to look upward to the sky. There it is—an aeroplane. Descending slowly, the pilot lands on the Circle C Ranch. The crowd waves in delight as the aeroplane makes a bumpy landing on uneven ground and comes to a stop.

Carlene Cortina triumphantly bounds out of her aeroplane to a cheering crowd. Mady Blaylock bounds onto her horse and unceremoniously leaves the party. With all eyes on the aeroplane, no one notices Mady's exit, including Centori.

Centori makes his way through the people who circled the aeroplane and welcomes the pilot with a warm embrace. Another cheer from the crowd. It is in earshot of the departing Mady.

"Welcome to the Circle C Ranch, Carlene. It is great to see you!"

"Thank you! That is quite a house and quite a crowd. I'm not surprised."

Griegos comes over and says, "Thanks for your help in our adventure. We could use you again for the fall roundup."

"This time I would provide aerial coverage for cattle. Isn't that right, Adobe?"

"Yes, we have run out of gold mines. Would you like a drink?"

"Sure."

"How about a Chimayo Whiskey?"

"I have heard about that drink, but never had one."

"It is reputed to be a very fortifying drink."

"Thank you," she says with no reaction to his description.

The merry-making continues into dusk.

***

As a beautiful moon over the high desert rises, Centori looks her in the eyes and says, "Carlene, it's getting late. Stay here tonight. We could fly again in the morning."

"Thank you, but I will be fine."

"Are you sure? It's too risky to fly in the twilight."

"Some risks are greater than others," she states with conviction.

"I wonder why?" he says with concern.

"A smart man learns not to wonder why a woman changes her mind."

He could hardly imagine a greater rejection. She nods and leaves without saying another word. He watches the rhythm of her gait. She looks up at the sky, but does not turn around. In matters of love, Adobe Centori seldom won, but he always tried. It is an end to a promising romance. He has never trusted happiness. He never did and he never will.

***

The last guest leaves and Centori retreats to his *sanctum sanctorum* to live through the inflicted wound of Carlene's rebuff. The Chimayo Whiskey dulls the physical pain of rejection, but the emotional pain remains. Sitting in a chair, he enters an in-between state where he is neither completely awake nor completely asleep, a place where sleep hallucinations can occur...

"*Mi corazon*, wake up," Gabriela says with resolve.

"No, I want to stay here with you," he says with resistance.

"Wake up. You cannot stay here. You must leave me and listen to my request."

Centori jumps up from his dream and tries to remember the request. He cannot.

The next night his dreamscape is strangely the same. Yet, with more focus.

"Wake up, *mi corazon*, wake up," she says in a white dress, eyes straight ahead and little purple flowers tumbling from her left hand.

"No, I want to stay with your love and your beauty."

"You cannot stay here. You must wake up now."

"Gabriela?"

"You must accept my request."

Centori emerges from his dream without memory of the request and feels an emotional void that seems impossible to fill. She has forever made an impression on his heart and spirit.

CHAPTER 57

SAN FELIPE DE NERI

A few days later, Centori arrives in Albuquerque to meet with the New Mexico Cattle Growers' Association. The meeting will be in Old Town, the original site of Albuquerque. The Spanish founded Old Town with the central plaza layout in the 1700s. The plaza is enclosed by adobe brick buildings and the San Felipe de Neri Church. The church, built in 1793, expands the entire north side of the plaza.

After the meeting to promote the economic health of the cattle industry, Centori walks near the church where a girls' choir sings in Spanish—and feels the peace that has eluded him since Gabriela's death. Although not religious, he is compelled to enter the church and light a candle to honor her memory. Leaving the church, he finds Patriot, rides back to the Circle C and tries to remember her request.

***

Suspended in midair, Gabriela grasps the silver cross that hangs around her neck and without a word of farewell falls to her certain death. That was the last earthly experience Centori ever had with her. Over the last few years, ghosts and dreams were communication conduits. Now, the dreams come more frequently with her mysterious request that continues to haunt him. Finally, he makes a big decision.

CHAPTER 58

HAVANA, CUBA

Centori meets Griegos at the horse barn and informs, "I am going on a trip, and it could take a week or more. As usual, the ranch is in your hands."

"Of course, but where are you going?"

"Back to Cuba."

"What for?"

"I would like to see how the country is handling independence from Spain and from the U.S."

"It has been many years since U.S. military rule ended," Griegos questions.

"A vacation then," Centori adds with some annoyance.

"Okay, Boss."

He will return to Cuba, the place where he met his one true love—perhaps he can find the meaning of her request.

***

One week later, Centori arrives in Havana and checks into Hotel Inglaterra, the oldest hotel in Cuba, on *Paseo del Prado*. The four-story building has a neoclassical design and a glass marquee.

Winston Churchill stayed at the hotel as a military reporter in 1895. In his room, Centori finds electricity, a telephone, a telegraph link and vivid memories. He recalls Gabriela's passion for Cuban independence that excited his imagination; her passionate embrace excited his romantic nature. He thinks of the first moment with her.

> It was a late summer day at the Plaza de Armas; he was drinking café Cubano and became intrigued with a woman sitting alone. She was Gabriela Zena, a stately, gracious and strong leader of an independence movement. She instinctively turned toward him and smiled. About her face was a splendid beauty that framed a charming smile, revealing a confident attitude. Gabriela's black hair was straight, long and wrapped in a band bearing the words Cuba Libre. The Cuban revolution had ended, yet when their eyes locked for the first time, a quiet revolution began in his heart.

A knock on the door interrupts his thoughts.
"Here are your bags, *Senor*."
"*Gracias*."
Instead of unpacking, Centori studies a street map of Havana, but drifts back to a memory. The full, silvery moon provided enough light to see the street sign: *Calle Vera Cruz*.

> Gabriela's house at number 48 was a stately two-story baroque structure. He stopped in front of a grand ornate door and looked up, absorbing the atmosphere. He then reflected on the words of Dante Alighieri: *Love with delight discourses in my*

mind, upon my lady's admirable gifts, beyond the range of human intellect. He knocked on the solid wood door and she opened it, smiling. "Good evening, Aldoloreto. Or should I call you Adobe?"

Centori never told anyone about the origin of his name. That night Adobe was born in more than one way and he was about to have the adventure of a lifetime. He returns to writing to Griegos, but a strong wind blows through the window, wildly shaking the curtains. He leaves the hotel to see the ground they strolled together some fifteen years ago.

Walking near a church, he hears a girls' choir singing in Spanish. He enters the church, lights a candle and hears, *I am your Guardian Angel, know my voice, be open to my signs. You will have true love again.*

At sunrise, Centori walks along the Havana Bay shore and receives a voice, but no one is around. The angelic, Spanish voice is singing a familiar melody—the same song as the girls' choir sang in San Felipe de Neri in Albuquerque.

***

Centori returns to the Circle C with a new perspective on his star-crossed romance. Gabriela has been reconciled with a new appreciation of her role in his life. There is every indication that he has achieved the peace that has long evaded him. However, there is one more thing to do—he will go to her unmarked grave in some far away, forgotten place.

***

At the spot in Chaco Canyon where she died, Centori finds the rocks that buried *La Guerrillera* and places little purple flowers on her grave. He speaks aloud expressing his everlasting love and feels a spiritual presence.

Then an ephemeral vision of Gabriela whispers, "*Mi corozon*, our time on earth ended too soon, but we will meet again. *Escucha mi voz.* You will find comfort in my request. I can see it in your eyes. You have come to understand and accept my wish—I am your angel, *vaya con Dios.*"

CHAPTER 59

VAGUE VILLA

By now, General Pershing has covered hundreds of miles of mountains and deserts inside Mexico with 6,000 soldiers in the pursuit of Pancho Villa. At the start, the Mexican Punitive Expedition succeeded in several engagements with Villista soldiers. In addition, The U.S. army engaged in skirmishes with President Carranza's federal forces.

Although Pershing found and defeated a large part of Villa's army, his force was unable to prevent Villa's escape. However, there were no further Villa raids on the United States. Pershing has not achieved the expedition's major objective: Villa remains elusive. Centori's decision not to join the chase may have been the right move.

Beyond Villa remaining active, Germany is watching the U.S. Army performance in Mexico with strategic interest. As a result, the Kaiser and his government view Pershing's army as lacking in military readiness and effectiveness.

An outcome is German Foreign Secretary Arthur Zimmerman's telegram to the German Ambassador in Mexico City. The telegram message proposed a German-Mexican alliance should the U.S. enter the Great War.

Based upon the U.S. performance in Mexico, the Kaiser is confident that Germany has a superior army. The alliance would return the vast Southwest area, lost in the Mexican War, to Mexico—a very ambitious plan.

CHAPTER 60

SEASONS

Spring turns to summer. While Adobe Centori has acquired new wealth in monetary form, there are no substantial changes to his life or to the Circle C Ranch.

Carmencita returned to her job at Mad Mady's Saloon with her dream of leaving Valtura for Los Angeles gone. She did not mention anything about Santa Fe Sharon to Mad Mady. Raphael disappeared, probably forever.

In June, raids on U.S. border towns continued. By August, more than 100,000 National Guardsmen reinforced the U.S. Army along the border in California, Arizona, New Mexico and Texas.

On the morning of July 1, 1916, British divisions went "over the top" and moved across "no-man's land near the Somme River in France. German machine guns opened up, killing more than 20,000 British soldiers with another 38,000 wounded—it was the largest single-day loss for the British army. The Battle of the Somme became synonymous with slaughter.

Summer turns to fall. As usual, in the fall roundup, the cowboys moved cattle to market by driving selected cattle to the stockyards and railheads. There was no aerial coverage of the range in search of mavericks, no aeroplane rides of any kind.

Fall turns to winter. In January, 1917, the British intercepted, and held, German foreign minister Arthur Zimmermann's coded message intended for the German ambassador in Mexico. Germany offered financial support and a military alliance—one that required Mexico to attack the United States. In this way, U.S. involvement in the European war would diminish if not end. In return, Mexico's lost Southwest territories would revert to Mexico.

In February, after a year of U.S. and Mexico relations deteriorating, Mexican President Carranza requested that Pershing withdraw from Mexico, bringing the two countries to the brink of war. Diplomacy between President Carranza and President Wilson avoided war.

As part of a negotiated settlement, U.S. soldiers departed Mexico. General Pershing's army did not capture Pancho Villa or ever see him. The chase ended. Most of the U.S. forces in Mexico returned to garrison duty at the border.

General Pershing, who emerged with a national profile, presented the Mexican Expedition as a success, despite not finding Villa. He believed that Wilson had too many constraints on the mission. That made it difficult, if not impossible, to capture Villa.

However, the pursuit demonstrated that America has the power to protect and defend its borders. Moreover, the Mexican Expedition provided training and experience should the U.S. enter the European war. The U.S. army gained vital logistical, field and operational knowledge. In some way, the withdrawal from Mexico reinforced Centori's decision not to join Pershing's army. The winds of the Mexican Punitive Expedition subsided. A far greater, unimaginable storm continues across the Atlantic and blows no good for America.

In the North Atlantic, Germany launched unrestricted submarine attacks on American ships. In March, news of the German plan to entreat Mexico to declare war on the U.S. and to attack Border States became public. Mexico would recover its territories lost in the Mexican-American war and the Gadsden Purchase: California, Nevada and Utah, parts of Arizona, Colorado and New Mexico. Mexico ignored the plan.

The Zimmermann telegram and then the sinking of three U.S. merchant ships by German U-boats were enough to break America's neutrality. The U.S. would enter into the First World War. The Zimmermann Telegram follows:

> We intend to begin on the first of February unrestricted submarine warfare. We shall endeavor in spite of this to keep the United States of America neutral. In the event of this not succeeding, we make Mexico a proposal of alliance on the following basis: make war together, make peace together, generous financial support and an understanding on our part that Mexico is to reconquer the lost territory in Texas, New Mexico, and Arizona. The settlement in detail is left to you. You will inform the President of the above most secretly as soon as the outbreak of war with the United States of America is certain and add the suggestion that he should, on his own initiative, invite Japan to immediate adherence and at the same time mediate between Japan and ourselves. Please call the President's attention to the fact that the ruthless employment of our submarines now offers the prospect of

compelling England in a few months to make peace. Signed, Zimmermann

One month later and two months after the Mexico operation, President Wilson ended the U.S. neutrality policy with a declaration of war against Germany on April 2, 1917—America would enter the Great War.

PART THREE

FRANCE

CHAPTER 61

UNCLEAR DESTINY

Adobe Centori rides in from the south, returning from Valtura and from seeing Mad Mady—their friendship settled into old familiar patterns. He dismounts and walks toward Francisco Griegos who is at the horse barn. Leading Patriot, Centori—with a troubled look on his face—approaches Griegos.

"What's wrong, Boss?"

"Wilson has gone and done it now—we are at war!"

"*Dios mio!* When?"

"On April 2nd he asked a joint session of Congress to declare war on Germany. A few days later, the Senate and the House provided overwhelming approval."

"I guess Wilson ran out of reasons to keep us out."

"He did for three years, in line with his re-election promise. Well, he kept us from being directly involved. England and France have secured American bank loans to buy U.S. war supplies."

"I am sure that is known in Berlin."

Centori nods, brings Patriot into the house barn and returns to say, "Things have changed. German U-boats are attacking

American merchant ships approaching Britain, resuming unrestricted ocean warfare."

"Germany must have known that action would bring the U.S. into the war."

"They should have known," Centori states. "The Kaiser probably sees the U.S. as an economic power, not a military power."

"That is a big mistake."

Centori removes his hat and says, "Perhaps our entry was inevitable."

Griegos wonders if Centori's enlistment in the army is inevitable.

"The Zimmermann telegram has changed Wilson and public opinion from neutrality to military action—and now to war. He said this war will make the world safe for democracy."

"You believe that?"

Centori closes the barn door and says, "I don't know, Francisco. I just don't know."

General Funston's death, after the Mexican Punitive Expedition, opened the door for General Pershing to command the American army in France. In May, President Wilson appointed Pershing as commander of the American Expeditionary Force (AEF). As a result, U.S. war preparation begins.

Despite the U-boat attacks and the Zimmerman telegram, the uncertainty about Wilson's declaration of war is shared by many Americans. The war is seen as another widespread imperial conflict across the continent that should not involve America.

Concerns about U.S. involvement in a European war relate to readiness. The U.S. military stands unprepared with 100,000 soldiers who are poorly equipped and lacking in tanks and aircraft. These deficiencies are in sharp contrast to Germany's highly professional and experience military.

The Kaiser's goal of a German-controlled European continent is far greater than Germany's goal in the limited 1870 Franco-Prussian War. The Kaiser is feared to go beyond dominating Europe: world domination.

General Pershing and a well-trained army are destined for France. The destiny of Adobe Centori, however, remains unclear.

CHAPTER 62

TOUGH 'OMBRES

August 1917

General Pershing and his army continue to prepare for war. Armies in the AEF consist of two or more corps. Two or more divisions fill a corps. One of the divisions is the 90th Infantry Division. Under the command of General Henry T. Allen, the 90th Division was activated. General Allen commanded a unit of the 11th Cavalry as part of Pershing's Mexican Punitive Expedition. The former National Guard unit is comprised of men mostly from Texas and Oklahoma as well as men from other states including New Mexico.

The insignia for the 90th Division is T.O. for Texas and Oklahoma. Their nickname, Tough 'Ombres, represents the *esprit de corps* of the division. General Pershing did not respond to Adobe Centori's request to receive a colonelship in the AEF— or provide any response at all. As a result, Centori appealed to General Allen who agreed to meet him at Camp Travis, Texas, named for Alamo commander W. B. Travis. He requested the rank of colonel in the 90th Division. He received the rank of major.

Training for the 90th Division began at Camp Travis. The men drilled in bayonet and target practice and in entrenching and tactical troop movement. From there, the division travelled to Camp Mills in Long Island, New York, where recruits from Camp Upton, also in Long Island, joined the unit.

***

In October, 1917 the U.S Army engaged the Germans on the line. The 1st Division was deployed in the trenches near the towns of Nancy and Lorraine. That small role would change dramatically. By the end of the year, four divisions were on the Western Front, training near Verdun.

In the following spring, American victories at the Battle of Cantigny and the Battle of Belleau Woods prompted Pershing to call for an independent U.S. Army. In addition, American Doughboys helped to stop the German army from entering Paris at the Second Battle of the Marne and at the Battle of Chateau-Thierry. In June, the 90th Division prepared for departure to France. The Tough 'Ombres will enter the European continent during the German offensive against Paris and the French counter offensive.

During the Atlantic voyage, the 90th Division avoided serious contact with German submarines. Some units sailed to France while most units docked in Southampton before crossing the English Channel to Cherbourg, France. On July 4, 1918, the 358th Infantry of the 176th Brigade paraded into Liverpool, England. The mayor provided a banquet for the doughboys—including Major Adobe Centori, commander of the 358th Infantry.

After arriving in France, Centori and his regiment travelled by train and foot to resume training north of Dijon in the Cote-d'Or Mountains, with headquarters located near Toul on the

Nancy Highway. In the small French towns, the doughboys had their first encounters with the French language and customs. The Americans are warmly welcomed while learning to *parlez-vous.*

The men train in anticipation of taking their place on the line. Centori is an effective leader in approach marching, problems of attack, problems of organization, passage of lines and attack with other units—soon he will test his skills on the Western Front.

In August 1918, the 90th Division relieved the 1st Division on the line. The Tough 'Ombres entered the front north of Toul and west of Remenauville, a town containing German outposts. The division works on trenches, wire, dugouts and emplacements, while preparing for the St. Mihiel offensive. Although the big American Offensive is top secret, there are signs, such as the 90th HQ and rear echelon units moving forward. To hide the offensive, action is restricted to the usual artillery fire, airplane patrol and reconnaissance to locate the enemy. Field artillery brigades and trench mortar batteries move into position,

Centori and his regiment occupy an old French trench to intercept German patrols. Leading one of the first patrols from the 90th Division lines, Centori and his men engage Germans from Remenauville. Amidst rifle fire and machine gun fire he suffers a significant shrapnel wound and is sent to an aid station.

CHAPTER 63

ROUEN, FRANCE

Adobe Centori wakes at high alert, breathing heavily with a fast heart rate, and quickly realizes his situation. Recognizing a distinctive hospital scent, he wills his pulse to slow.

He shifts in his bed seeking more comfort from the pain of ripped flesh. Then he remembers that the Battle of St. Mihiel was in its final planning stages; he would need to return to his men.

The ancient city of Rouen in northern France is the capital of Normandy. Located on the River Seine, it was large and affluent in medieval Europe. Rouen has many half-timbered buildings: wood frames with exposed structural timbers and intervals full of bricks and stones.

There are remarkable buildings in Rouen and many remains of the French Renaissance. Notre Dame Cathedral with its gothic architecture and the Rouen Castle with its *tour Jeanne d'Arc*, provide striking images of the French built environment. Gothic buildings, castles and churches such as Church of St. Maclou and the Church of Ouen reflect eternity. In a country as old as France, it is difficult to be neutral to the beauty of the architectural treasures.

Rouen, a center for military base hospitals, is located miles behind the battle lines and within reasonable range of the ambulance trains. Base hospitals are a key link in the evacuation chain for wounded soldiers. In the spring of 1918, doughboys began to arrive at the hospitals after the first American offensive at the Battles of Cantigny and Belleau Woods.

Centori finds himself within General Hospital No. 8. Located in the southern part of the city, it is the largest base hospital in Rouen. Within a frenzied hospital that is loud with activity, he is one of many soldiers in need of medical attention. He takes a deep breath, braces himself as an eye-catching nurse with an attractive profile draws a metal shard from his shoulder. She turns to present a straight nose and a full mouth that give her a regal look. Reflectively, with a touch of intrigue, she moves her eyes. She administers to the wound and hands him a bandage and a tired smile before quickly moving away, offering no soft-spoken words of encouragement. Her sparkling brown eyes and glowing skin provide a satisfying substitute for him.

Focusing on her interesting image in uniform, Centori compresses the linen bandage, flinches, then slowly turns to see the removed shard in a metal dish. The shrapnel wound starts to close and a slight stream of blood flows. Lingering in the same position, he reaches to soothe his shoulder and discovers a dreadful void—the silver medallion is gone.

Amid the chaotic hospital, a melodious voice speaks in a low tone, *"Coment tu te sens?"*

Beyond a charming face and figure, he finds her voice to be particularly pleasant and her French accent adds enchantment. Surprised by the rapid return of an angel in a white uniform, Centori sits up and offers full attention, "Yes, well enough."

Their eyes meet for a second as she replies, *"Tres bien."*

Ignoring his pain, he says, "Well enough to be released. I need to return to my unit immediately."

"We shall make that determination in a day or two, but for now you must accept your situation."

She steps away and trips over a pile of discarded uniforms. Losing her balance, she stumbles against a table, a metal tray crashes and clangs on the floor. Her cap slips, revealing falling auburn hair. Centori rushes over to help; she is in his arms sooner than hoped. He quickly straightens with a gesture embedded within his personality.

About the same height, their eyes squarely meet. They stare at each other until his gaze dips down to her feet and quickly up again. This subtle assessment would have made her aware of the less than flattering white outfit—if she had the time. She takes a swift breath and remains as still as a statue, surprised but not enthralled by his daring.

"Thank you, but you should stay in bed. You could reopen your wound."

They share a moment, at least from his perspective. He sees a promise that she had no intention of making, "Will I see you again, Nurse?" he asks with assertion.

Seemingly startled, she replies, "At the earliest possible time."

"That could be next to never," he says and realizes it is not a good time to talk.

"C'est la vie," she declares with a defensive posture. Then she proudly lifts her head and walks away.

Disappointed, he hopes his presence will be hard to ignore. Then, he realizes that the Silver Medallion he had since Calabaza give it to him is gone.

"Nurse," he calls out.

She turns toward him.

"I was wearing a medallion with American Indian symbols around my neck."

"Yes, your personal belongings are secure," she assures him in a polite tone.

"Thank you. I would like to have it back as soon as possible."

"I understand. *Au revoir.*"

On another day or during another time, she may have been receptive, but today she could not have cared less. She is too insensitive, the only way to survive her highly sensitive job. Unfazed, the seriousness of the situation propels her back to her duties. He watches the sway of her hips as she walks away. Centori's overture failed to obtain a rendezvous, but he may have gained her curiosity.

CHAPTER 64

WAR NURSE

The next day, Centori shifts in his bed, anxiously awaiting a certain nurse. Despite his wound, he is strong and alert. Here she comes.

In a vague way, she looks prettier today than yesterday. She acts as though their moment never happened and asks, "How are you today?"

"Better now. You should smile more often."

She looks at the American with a ghost of a grin, "There is not much to smile about these days."

Despite the rebuff, he is reassured and replies, "Of course, you are right."

She reaches into a pocket and pulls out the silver medallion, "I believe this is the American Indian item you seek," her voice less harsh.

"Yes, thank you very much."

Holding the artifact by its chain, she says, "It is very beautiful. Are the symbols significant?"

Delighted by the interest, he answers, "Yes. Historical significance, dating to when the Spanish arrived in the American Southwest."

"I see. It is beautiful and interesting. I have news for you, Major. You will be released today."

"*Merci.*"

"You can rejoin your men. Do be careful. I hope not to see you in hospital again."

"I hope to see you away from here," he proclaims boldly.

"*Pour qui est-ce que tu me prends?*"

He shakes his head in confusion.

"What do you think I am? *Ce que tu proposes est incroyable!* What you propose is unimaginable."

"Would it be so bad?" he asks and searches her face for changed emotions.

With a suggestion of a smile, she answers, "That would be neither bad nor good."

"If not good or bad, then what is it?"

"Just out of the question. *Au revoir!*"

As she walks away, he calls out, "May I know your name?"

She turns with the coolness of a war nurse and replies, "Elodie."

A hopeful smile appears on Centori's face. He could have her respect, but affection is a far reach. She appears stirred by this soldier, but it could be gratitude for a liberating American.

***

Elodie Saint-Sauveur volunteered to be part of the war, part of the exhausting, dangerous and stressful base hospital work. All the nurses are dealing with the terrible medical demands of battle. Wounded men arrive at all times, day and night. Nurses stay on their feet for an entire shift, which can be a grueling twelve hours—and stay close to the wounded during air raids. Many nurses feel isolated as No. 8, surrounded by gray stone walls, is located away from other units and from the town. Despite the extreme hardships, the nurses are the face of the hospitals. Given the level of care administered, many soldiers say a nurse saved them.

Although Nurse Saint-Sauveur suffers the harsh conditions, she is somewhat different from the other nurses. Born in the fashionable 7th *Arrondissement* of Paris, she is the only child of affluent parents. She is well bred with *savior faire* but she is not too fine for hard work. Educated in the fine arts, with expertise in art history, she graduated from *École des Beaux-Arts*, an influential Paris art school with worldwide appeal. John Mervan Carrere and Thomas Hasting, who studied at the French school, designed the New York Public Library, an architectural spectacle. Before the war, she worked at the *Musee des Beaux-Arts* as a museum director and art historian. Elodie has expertise as an archivist and curator. She is a highly capable keeper of French cultural heritage in painting and sculpture.

As part of the *bourgeoisie*, her family was financially successful. Although some describe capital ownership as materialistic, it powers the economic engine. Critics may have driven Elodie to enter a profession that serves people.

Centori is not among those who would criticize the *bourgeoisie*– and is certainly unlikely to find fault in her. Elodie Saint-Sauveur has resisted the touch of a man; she is single, independent and outwardly content.

CHAPTER 65

TRENCHES

It is not long before Major Centori returns to the frontline trenches to resume command of the 358th Infantry regiment. The elation of leaving the hospital faded once he was within the grim reality of the trenches—and then there was that nurse. German artillery shells, mortars, poison gas and machine gun fire are commonplace at the front. Attacks are not the only form of dreadfulness. Conditions in the trenches are breeding grounds for many diseases.

Soldiers in the trenches rotate back and forth between the frontline and reserve trenches, usually in six-day intervals to provide periods of rest. Less frequently, soldiers receive leaves to recover or to see wounded friends in the hospital. When possible, Centori will avail himself of the policy in hopes of seeing a certain nurse.

On the Western Front, millions of men live in trenches with their steel helmets just below the sandbagged parapets. Communication trenches are used to move soldiers to and from the front. Dugouts, large areas scratched out of the trenches, are for the use of one or a few men.

Alone in his dugout command post, Centori takes a hidden cognac bottle and looks at the correspondence concerning the first American offensive. After achieving his military goal, he drafts a letter concerning his romantic goal.

"Welcome back, Major."

Centori looks up to find Captain Romero of Company B at the dugout entrance saluting.

"Thanks," he answers while returning the salute.

"How's the shoulder?"

"It's fine. It was a bad time to get hurt with D-Day coming."

"It's never a good time."

"Of course, you are right."

"I hope to go to Rouen on my next leave," Captain Romero says.

"I am thinking about returning to Rouen. There is someone I would like to see there."

"A woman?"

Centori nods and says, "I may never see her again anyway."

At the same time, General Pershing prepares for a large-scale operation of the first American Offensive.

CHAPTER 66

RENDEZVOUS

Adobe Centori did not expect to see Elodie Saint-Sauveur again, but he wished. By some fortune of love or war, she answered his letter. Perhaps curiosity got the best of Elodie; she knows little about this interesting foreigner. Perchance, he is a man worth knowing.

At the appointed time, Centori waits in the shadow of the Gothic Notre-Dame de l'Assomption de Rouen Cathedral. He strains to see her in the crowd. *How will she look in civilian clothes?* he thinks while noticing French women walking in dresses that reflect need not style. With more women working, fashion became better suited for work. In addition, the severity of war resulted in darker colors and shorter dresses with simple tailoring to be common.

Unlike England or Germany, the French home front is close to the battle lines. The trenches on the Western Front are in northern France and Belgium, with Rouen painfully close to the battlefields. There is music in the distance. Now it is clear, *La Marsellaise*. The French national anthem sounds Elodie's arrival, he likes to think. On the other hand, is it the ringing of the cathedral bells marking the hour and her presence? In any case, she accepted an invitation for a rendezvous. Here she comes.

"Elodie, thank you for meeting me."

"Major Centori, you selected a lovely place to meet."

"Please call me Adobe," he says, appreciating her somewhat fashionable dress and hat with a broad face-shadowing brim. From under her hat, eyes promise more than she would deliver. She notices how dashing he looks in his worn uniform buttoned up to the high collar.

"I admire architecture," he says. "This cathedral is a marvel. It reminds me of the design of New York's Woolworth Building. In fact, that building is called the Cathedral of Commerce."

"I see, and how old is the Woolworth Building?"

"It's a new building just a few years old."

"The Rouen Cathedral has been here since the 12th century!"

"Somewhat older," he smiles, "The Woolworth is the tallest building."

"Our cathedral was the tallest in the late 19th century with the addition of the lantern tower. Look at the beautiful stained glass."

"I feel like I know this building."

She smiles in agreement, "Perhaps you have seen the cathedral paintings by Claude Monet. There are several, each representing different lighting and weather conditions."

"Perhaps I have."

"How is your shoulder?" she asks with a light touch.

"Better now."

"I see."

"Thank you again for coming. I know you are busy at the hospital."

"Your profession keeps my profession *very* busy."

Unsure how to respond, he says, "I am glad you had time to see me."

"Not much time. Shall we walk?"

Without hesitation, he presents his arm and she accepts. They walk in silence and appear comfortable in an awkward situation. Yet, the interaction does not require words; any affection is implicit.

There are many people out walking, trying to forget the war for a time. The sound of other voices and activities are indistinct as the shadows extend. As she slows her pace slightly, he carefully admires every move she makes. She feels beautiful in his gaze. He notices a slight spring in her breasts.

A little later, Elodie urges a left turn, stirring him from comforting thoughts. They enter a small square with several cafes where men are drinking coffee and smoking cigarettes. They pass a *pâtisserie* and admire the limited pastries in the window; next door is a *boulangerie* with baguettes and hearty bread. Beyond that is her favorite café and the smell of coffee and croissants.

In *Café Cheri*, they find an inviting round table with two chairs next to an open window. She has a *café au lait*; he has a *café noir*. They both have *pain au chocolat*.

"This is good coffee," he says, unsure if it is the aroma or the taste. It stirs his senses and reminds him of Cuban coffee and another woman, but only for a second.

"This is much better than army coffee."

"You are becoming enamored with France," she quips.

"I am becoming enamored with you," he declares brazenly.

Mildly embarrassed, she asks, "Do you have a family in America?"

"Some in New York, I guess, but my real family is in New Mexico."

She stirs a spoon in her cup and asks, "You are not an American?"

"I am an American from the 47th state of the United States!"

"Ah, the American West. So you are a cowboy, no?"

"I am a cowboy, yes!"

"A cowboy with an interesting Indian medallion."

Centori pauses and says, "That's right. It was discovered on my ranch."

"That is indeed intriguing."

He reaches into his tunic and presents the silver medallion, "It is hundreds of years old."

She smiles her approval and says, "It is beautiful too."

"What is the name of your ranch?"

"I christened it the Circle C."

"I like that name. Before the war, I saw American photoplays with cowboys and ranches—such a big beautiful country."

"Watching the stars in the enormous western sky is wonderful. Each star is like a jewel arrayed across an endless dark silk canvas."

"It sounds stunning."

"Very much so. New Mexico is larger than the U.K. but has a small population of about 350,000, most live in our largest city, Albuquerque."

"You love to talk about New Mexico."

"I suppose I do...colorful canyons are miraculous. Coyote cries are haunting. Sometimes I feel they are calling me. I know that's foolish."

"Not so foolish, I think that is special. Why would *cohoote* not want to talk to you?"

"Ha, *cohoote*, your accent needs improvement. Elodie, it is nice to be with you and away from the terrible war."

"It is nice to be away from the hospital."

He frowns faintly.

She tries to suppress the thought, but says, "Yes, of course... here with you too."

They engage in expansive talks about many things in the world, except the world war.

CHAPTER 67

ST. MIHIEL SALIENT

Under General Pershing's leadership, the U.S. First Army with seven divisions will attack the salient at St. Mihiel, a German strong point that resisted previous attacks. The salient contains a double line of trenches, barbed wire and pillboxes; beyond is the formidable famous Hindenburg Line. The offensive will be the sole responsibility of the Americans. In preparation of the Battle of St. Mihiel, the Americans coin the terms "D-Day" and "H-Hour."

In this first massive offensive under American leadership, the First Army will attack to evacuate the St. Mihiel Salient. The German position, almost 30 miles wide, protrudes miles into allied lines. General Pershing characterized the defenses as a field fortress, but both flanks could be attacked at once.

Railroad and communication lines are in place. Aviation, artillery and tank units, and supply depots are ready. Medical, engineering and military police units are poised to serve the offensive. Almost 220,000 doughboys are on the line, with 190,000 in reserve. French soldiers on the line number some 50,000.

Three divisions of the First Army Corps will attack—including the 90th Infantry Division, positioned at the extreme right. The mission of the 90th Division is to protect the right flank of advance.

The American Sector aims to reduce the salient, relieve the French forces at Verdun and capture the Verdun-Toul-Belfort railroad. The attack of four army corps, commanded by General Fuchs, will pinch the salient and cut off the retreating Germans.

This first American-led operation, the largest offensive ever commenced by the U.S. Army, is a grand challenge for the doughboys that will test the men of the AEF, including the 90th Infantry Division.

CHAPTER 68

RENDEZVOUS REDUX

Returning to Rouen, Centori meets Elodie at the *Café Cheri*. They take the same table and order *café au lait* and *café noir*. At first, he was reluctant to leave the front, given the impending St Mihiel operation. He settled the internal conflict with a much shorter stay behind the lines, but long enough to see her again.

Centori stares into his cup and she reacts by saying, "Are you feeling bad?"

Having learned a costly lesson by trusting German spy Jennifer Prower, he dares not mention the source of his distraction: St.Mihiel. Instead, he offers, "I am fine. I would like to see *Palais de Justice* today."

"*Oui.* I will to show you the *Palais de Justice* and the great art museums of Rouen."

***

After coffee and *pain au chocolat*, they leave the *café* to explore Rouen. At the *Palais de Justice*, the heart of history, they view the ornate Gothic architecture that expresses its 16th century glory. At the *Musee des Beaux-Arts de Rouen*, they enjoy the visual art, including the paintings of Delacroix, Renior, Pissarro, Degas and Monet.

They stroll through the galleries. Elodie stops at a Monet painting: *Les coteaux pres de Vetheuil* (Rocky Landscape near Vetheuil) a painting of wandering river banks on the Seine. She stares at the painting.

Centori notes the odd behavior and says, "I assume you like Monet."

Elodie, as motionless as the painting, utters, "I wish we could freeze this day. What amazing evocation of certain emotions. Is this painting magic or amusement?"

He looks askew at her and adds, "There are strong parallels between magic and art."

"Parallels that are intimate, when viewed aesthetically. Perhaps there are ulterior motives that make it desirable to express certain emotions and not others emotion."

She whispers something in French. The meaning of the words are unknown to him.

"I love the opera," he says. "The music I listen to is not what comes out of the Victrola—rather that sound as altered by my imagination."

"*Oui*. That can be said about all the arts," she expresses. "However, the outcome of 'a work of art' depends on whether the effect is magical or amusing."

Once again, she whispers in French. The meaning is unknown to him, but this time the tone is clear. This French woman further intrigues him.

"*Alors*, when a woman expresses an emotion. She is aware of that emotion but unsure of its meaning. All she feels is the excitement within her and from this condition she expresses herself."

Then she presents slightly separated lips; it was enough for him. He gently touches her cheek, causing her neck to tip back. Abruptly, she leads him by the hand; she knows her way around the vast building.

At a brisk pace, they enter a deserted stairwell and throw caution to the wind. He looks around before kissing her. Elodie pulls up her dress and pulls down her undergarments. He steps back, taking in the sight before the embrace; it takes a moment before he takes her in his arms. Pressed against a wall in a public place, her passion is intensified by the enormity of the risk.

"Elodie, Elodie? Are you okay?"

"Yes, of course. Why do you ask?"

"You seemed frozen in place, mesmerized by the painting," he studies her face.

"Perhaps a little uncomfortable," she says, retreating from her fantasy.

"Let's sit down here."

In front of *Les coteaux pres de Vetheuil*, he repeats, "I asked if you like Monet and you were distant."

"Yes, I do...Monet...yes of course, about this painting."

Elodie provides a lecture on Monet with such energy that any previous daydream could not stand a chance in her mind. "Of course, Monet the French impressionist was great in painting perceptions. The very term comes from his painting *Impression, soleil levant* or Impression Sunrise."

"Elodie, are you okay?"

"Yes, why do you ask?"

"No reason."

She continues her breathless discourse, "He used a painting style that captured the same scene several times, thus expressing the changing light and changing seasons."

Monet created great landscaping around his home; it featured lily ponds, which inspired his water lily paintings. Elodie created a great impossible fantasy right before Centori's very eyes.

CHAPTER 69

TRENCHES

Back in the trenches, Centori finds the distance from Elodie to be an added hardship to the stress of war. At times, it is a most unbearable situation. The dark distance across the Western Front adds to the perfumed barrier that prevents him from entering her bed. A barrier that creates a strange delight of being separated, and so he misses her more.

Sitting at his command post in the dugout, Centori takes the cognac bottle and thinks of Elodie, *I miss her beauty, the way she sounds speaking English, and her engaging and caring conversations. Yet, something about her behavior while standing in front of the painting is puzzling. How strange she was that day.* He looks at this watch, *Time to go.* Elodie will take a back seat to his meeting with the high command and subsequent meetings with his company commanders.

His next rotation from the front is approaching; he will lose no time in returning to Rouen, he has no time to lose. There will be time for one more visit to Rouen before D-Day. Then, he becomes determined to study the St. Mihiel battle plan, before his company commanders arrive. The First Army supported by Allied artillery and tanks will launch an attack on the 25-mile-wide strongpoint. If a breakthrough occurs, the plan calls for the capture of Metz and to envelope the salient with a pincer movement, driving the Germans back to the Hindenburg line.

Captain Romero arrives with the other six company commanders.

"Come in," Centori says.

The men gather around and Centori refers to reports and says, "Before we attack, the location of German trenches, troop strength, strongpoints, and machine gun and mortar positions for our sector will be determined."

"We are expecting reports from our patrols."

"When?"

"Before sunrise," Romero answers.

"We all know that this information is vital to infantry movements and artillery attacks."

"Yes, Major Centori," Captain MuCuloch of Company A acknowledges.

"Good. In addition, roads, depots and telephone locations must appear on our intelligence maps," Centori says, reaching for the cognac bottle.

As he pours a round of short drinks, he asks, "Has anyone heard about Colonel Patton?"

Captain Larson of Company C answers, "He will lead a cavalry-style tank attack!"

"Those tanks should surprise the German infantry, giving us an advantage," Romero says.

An artillery shell rocks the dugout, sending the men diving for cover. All stand up and brush themselves off. Centori looks at his shaken company commanders and says, "Let's meet again in a half hour."

***

Centori and his captains continue their meeting and absorb Field Order Number 9, First Army, AEF, dated September 7, 1918:

The First Army will attack at H hour on D day with the object of forcing the evacuation of the St. Mihiel Salient

CHAPTER 70

SOIXANTE QUINZE

Adobe Centori is a long way from New Mexico; the Circle C Ranch is far from his thoughts. Other things are on his mind as he moves through narrow streets lined with cobblestones and centuries-old buildings with slanted roofs. The First Army will attack at H-hour on D-day. He has less than six hours before he returns to the front. All things are in place to force the evacuation of the St. Mihiel Salient. He will spend the lull before the storm in Rouen—and with Elodie.

Rouen has many disjointed, indirect streets and closed ended alleys. Stone buildings show centuries of exposure to the elements, including a Norman church surrounded by medieval walls. He halts in his stride to admire the structure and magnificent stained-glass windows.

Centori finds Elodie's two-story stone house, stops at its strong wooden door and notices windows with faded red shutters. Even before she appears, he feels encircled in a slim floral scent of fine French perfume. She pulls the door open with some struggle. Her fragrance and her pale-green Gingham dress are inviting. In full flourish, Elodie stands as a figure filled with elegance, a flower in bloom.

"*Bonsoir, Bienvenue a ma maison.*"

"*Mademoiselle, je vous remercie. Vous etes tres jolie ce soir!*"

She finds his attempt at French humorous, "Your pronunciation is terrible."

"Guess, I'll have to learn to *parlez-vous*," he quips, "or stick with an international language."

Ignoring the indelicate comment, she ushers, "*Entrez, s'il vous plait!* er, come right in please."

In the parlor, where large tapestries adorn the stark walls, she offers, "*Vous voudriez une boisson;* er, would you like a cocktail?"

"*Oui, mademoiselle,*" he accepts as candlelight catches her beautiful face.

She moves toward her bar and continues, "This cocktail is known as a *Soixante Quinze* or 75."

"Is that right, I thought the French are partial to champagne," he says, unbuttoning his tunic.

"*Alors,* there are two times the French drink champagne: when happy and when sad. The *Soixante Quinze* contains gin, lemon juice, sugar—and champagne."

"I see," he smiles.

"Please sit while I prepare our drinks."

Settling into a Louis XV armchair, he studies the shape of her body as she walks away. Then, he studies the artistic tapestries on the stucco walls.

Close to him on a small table is a copy of *Madame Bovary* by Gustave Flaubert. The story is set in Normandy. After the adulterous Emma marries Charles Bovary, she starts an affair and becomes ill when her lover ends the affair. Another affair ends in despair, driving Emma to take arsenic and die.

Before he can wonder about her taste in books, she returns with two glasses and a cheese plate on a silver tray and says, "This strong drink is compared to the French 75mm artillery piece. It is a powerful potion of gin and champagne. Do be careful."

"I think I can handle it," says the Irish whiskey drinker.

"*Mais oui*," Elodie reacts while lifting her glass to her mouth, "Cheers."

"To victory!"

She takes no visible notice of the unwelcomed reminder. They click glasses and sip the fancy cocktail.

"Do you like the *Soixante Quinze?*"

"Yes, especially since you made it."

"*Va bon*," she says with a smile.

Both take another slow sip.

"Have you tried this Camembert cheese? It is a soft creamy cheese, created in the 18th century at Camembert, Normandy."

He takes a piece, lies about liking the fancy cheese and does not take another piece. Looking into his blue eyes, she reluctantly admits to herself that this American is magnetic. He meets the glance as her character, manner and intelligence come into focus.

Viewing elegant furniture, fine porcelain, stately fireplaces and chandeliers, he observes, "The ancient beauty of your house is extraordinary."

"Thanks to my family," she states quickly.

This is the home of a prosperous French family, he thinks while marveling and memorizing the parlor to relive it in the future.

She planned an elusive account of her life, but it came out, "The war has damaged the standard of living for most of the French, but not for all. Perhaps my family was fortunate. When the war began, the Germans captured industrial regions of France, partially destroying the economy."

American supplies, money and doughboys, stimulated the economy, he thinks but says, "Yes, you are fortunate. Your tapestries are imaginative."

"If I may say, I find your medallion to be quite artistic as well."

Since she wants to change the subject, he pauses and asks, "Would you like to see it again?"

"Yes, I was wondering."

Unbuttoning the tunic, he exposes the Silver Medallion.

Elodie, no stranger to art, conducts a close examination, "It is very beautiful. What do the symbols mean?"

"They are depictions of a geographical region in New Mexico."

"It must have much meaning to you."

"Although it was made centuries ago, it represents a place on my ranch."

"Your ranch must be special," she probes.

"Romantic too. The mountain views from my house are magnificent. Sunrise over the mountains and sunset on the mesa are beautiful."

"As I say, you love to talk about New Mexico! You are a proud and honorable cowboy...I remember an American photoplay with an honorable cowboy."

"You are probably thinking of William S. Hart."

"*Oui*! Are you like him? Are you the same?"

"Well, I am not like the desperados in his shows."

"Desperados?"

"Villains or criminals."

"Oh, I hope not," she smiles.

"I like your American Theda Bara and her photoplays."

"Have you seen her latest, *Madama Du Barry*?" he inquires.

"No. Unfortunately, we are too busy for such things, but the story is from a Dumas novel, *Memoirs d'un médecin*; an excellent book."

"I have not read that book, but I will now."

"Madame Du Barry, like Marie Antoinette, did not have a happy ending."

"We need more happy endings."

Elodie frowns at the reminder of the war and pivots, "I have something a cowboy would love," she ventures, "Would you like to see it?"

His decision is quick, "*Mais oui.*"

"Please follow me. We can see the beauty of this ancient house."

"Yes, I can already see that."

She leads the way into a wide hall lined with busts of Marat, Rousseau and Voltaire on one side and small tapestries decorating the opposite wall. They pass mysterious, ancient doors, perhaps bedrooms. Then they enter an art gallery with beautiful paintings that seem to contain several from the Old Masters.

"This is impressive," he declares, in an attempt to conceal an unlikely expectation.

Elodie points to a very large painting, "This is *Le marché aux chevaux, The Horse Fair,* by French artist, Rosa Bonheur."

"It is magnificent!"

"Do you know her work?"

"No, I am not familiar with this artist."

"She created this painting from a series of her drawings made at the Paris Horse Market. What brilliant naturalism of the horses."

"You are right; a cowboy would love this painting."

"It is considered her best work and it made her famous!"

"It is probably her largest too," he remarks, while gazing at the details of the fine horses.

"The original, at eight-feet high and 16-feet wide, is in the Metropolitan Museum of Art. Perhaps you have noticed it in New York."

"No, but it would not be better than seeing it here, with you at my side."

"*Ma mère et mon père* purchased this reproduction before I was born. It was the *de riguer* of sorts. Look how beautiful she infuses life into the canvas. They loved it so; I keep it in their memory."

After a tour of the other paintings, she asks, "Shall we return to the parlor?"

"*Oui, mademoiselle*," he agrees.

They walk silently through the hallway and return to their drinks.

"Have you had a French smoke?" she asks.

"No."

"Have this *Gauloises*," she says while extending her hand.

Very different from a *Romeo and Juliette*, but he accepts, unlikely to refuse anything from her. "You are full of surprises."

He lights the short, wide smoke that immediately reveals a strong aroma; she does the same.

"Elodie, I can see from the busts in the hallway that you are a patriot," he offers, "The English nurse Edith Cavell said patriotism is not enough."

"I understand...and with no limits in helping others in dire need."

"Edith Cavell was a great inspiration to me."

"She had an unfortunate end."

"Unfortunate? She was arrested and shot by a German firing squad for treason, even though she was not a German. I hate the Hun. They are brutal foes of civilization."

"A tragic end. I read the account. She helped many soldiers escape from occupied Belgium with false documents."

"Germany is an aggressor—they used poison gas in the trenches and aerial attacks on civilians in London! Yes, I hate the Hun."

"If the reports about the Germans executing civilians in Belgium at the start of the war are half-true, then Germany is clearly a brutal aggressor. Of course, the submarine attack on the *Lusitania* is completely true."

Elodie stops and wonders and then she says, "*Alors*, what moves an American cowboy to come across the ocean to fight for strangers?"

Thoughtful for a moment, he answers, "When we arrived in France, our rally cry was 'Lafayette, we are here' because the French were allies during our revolution when the British were winning. More accurately, when America was losing until the French arrived in America. So, Elodie we are here—I am here."

"Is that all?"

He gives her no further reply.

"Enough talk of war tonight," she declares.

Centori takes the statement as an invitation to more intimate topics. It was not. Elodie stands indicating the evening has ended. To his disappointment, the message is as apparent as if distinctly articulated.

"*Bonne nuit.*"

***

Centori rides the rails back to his regiment. The evening ended with Elodie staring into his eyes, clearly indicating that it was time to say good night. The night had a slight hint of impropriety and no French kiss. Elodie remains a woman who is completely in control of her sexual characteristics.

CHAPTER 71

BATTLE OF ST. MIHIEL

September 1918

One hour past midnight on September 12, 1918, thousands of allied guns roar against the salient. Allied aircraft provide additional support. Batteries open fire, signaling the start of the first American offensive and battle objective: reduce the Saint Mihiel Salient.

The First American Army, with a half-million doughboys, 100,000 French soldiers, 3,000 big guns and 250 tanks attack the salient. Supported by artillery and tanks, they will advance on the 25-mile-wide German strongpoint. Then, the men go over the top and encounter a dangerous maze of wire and hostile fire. Texas, Oklahoma, and New Mexico men, familiar with barbed wire, found the wire-cutter an important tool in no man's land to counter blocked defensives. When artillery and tanks fail to destroy all the wire, the doughboys improbably marched through the obstacles.

The first assaults are met with strong resistance. Major Centori's regiment starts to move up a bluff to take German trenches in the *Foret des Vencheres*, but they are met by machine gun fire. Captain Romero is immediately killed. Upon seeing his friend fall, Centori removes his insignia of rank, leaves his command post. He takes over Romero's company to lead an advance against German machine gunners.

Centori and his command flank the machine gun position and attack. His men fire their rifles as he empties his automatic pistol—eleven Germans are killed. The Tough 'Ombres continue to receive casualties from severe machine gun fire, but continue to advance towards their objectives

The next day, the doughboys entered the French village of Vigneulles. The 90th Division and the other divisions defeated the Germans along that front. It was a successful entry into the war for Major Centori and all the Tough 'Ombres. The American doughboys have far less battle experience than the Germans, but that did not matter.

In reaction to the American advance, the enemy retreated and burned villages in their path. The doughboys began digging trenches for their new positions—phase one is done.

CHAPTER 72

BREAKTHROUGH

Under a cloudy night sky, Centori peeps over the top into no-man's land. Most of the devastation is not visible at night. For a moment, the quiet battleground reminds him of the open spaces of New Mexico—but for only a moment. There is concern about a German counterattack.

He returns to his dugout and sits near the communication area. Reviewing the casualty reports, he stops to begin a letter to Captain Romero's mother. This leads to a reach for the cognac bottle.

Then he thinks of Elodie. The last time he saw her could be the last. Every rotation to the front could be his last. It was known that their future is anything but secure. She could easily become one with him, yet even if he survived the war, he would ultimately return to America. She believes that they could go their separate ways. She may be right.

The next morning, The Germans launch a counterattack. An artillery battalion of the 90th Division, that moved forward, helped to defeat the counter-attack. Along with the other divisions, the 90th is ordered to conduct raids. Once again, Centori removes his insignia of rank and leads his 1st Battalion. Crossing two bands of wire, they capture prisoners and important information about the famous Hindenburg line.

An Allied breakthrough happened on September 27: the Hindenburg Line near Cambriai and St. Quentin was breached. General Pershing declared the salient closed with the Americans in control of the field—removing the four-year-old bulge in German territory on the Western Front.

It cost the Allies 7,000 casualties. There were German counterattacks, but the doughboys secured the area and captured 250 guns, 15,000 Germans, reduced the salient, and were there to stay. More than 200 square miles of French territory was recaptured. The next job was to capture the land between the river and the forest. American troops advanced over the course of weeks, albeit with 75,000 casualties. Then, the Germans entrenched in the Argonne Forest. Logistical problems with supplies hampered the large-scale operation. Metz was not captured; the Germans entrenched and the Americans looked at the Argonne Forest. In the end, the Battle of St. Mihiel raised the stature of the U.S. Army. This victory was an overture to the last great battle of the war: the Meuse-Argonne.

CHAPTER 73

BLACK NEGLIGÉE

Inside Elodie's spacious bedchamber, candles burn on a dressing table and the *couvre-lit* is recklessly turned down. Sitting at the foot of the bed, she rests her hands and head on a bedpost. Walking to the large windows, where a candle on the table reflects in the window glass, she pulls the drapes and drops her robe to the floor. Turning to a large mirror, she admires the naked image while applying fine French perfume.

Candlelight illuminates an exposed body, and her eroticism, as she reaches across the bed. The soft light reveals a slim waist, curvy hips and stunning long legs. Skillfully, she drapes a black negligée over her body. A breath is drawn, causing her breasts to slightly expand the negligée; any remaining second thoughts are gone.

Elodie gently rocks herself to sleep where self-consciousness is abated, second thoughts suppressed, internal constraints shattered. As an aware dreamer, she invites him into her mind, ready to control her eroticism and exclaims, "*Entrez, s'il vous plait!*"

In her dreamscape, he quickly inhales at the sight of Elodie's inspirational outfit, enchanting fragrance and elegant body.

With curious eyes, she admires his uncanny charm as the most handsome man she had ever known.

Standing in an exquisite black negligée she offers, "*Vous voudriez une boisson?*" "*Oui, mademoiselle.*"

The drinks were placed in a far corner, allowing her to move seductively across the room.

"You remember this cocktail, *Soixante Quinze.*"

"Not as much as I remember you."

They sip and smile; her smile fades as his hands slip under the negligée straps.

"Elodie, I cannot resist a moment longer."

"Nor can I."

"I want to love you."

"Yes, please do, as much as you want."

He draws closer, eager to discover if French women are especially skillful in the art of lovemaking. Placing one arm on her shoulder and the other on her lower back, he gently pulls her closer. She feels more feminine than ever before, more excited than ever before, more beautiful than ever before. He kisses her neck, the French perfume intoxicating. A lustful caress, filled with potential for powerful passion, causes her to tremble.

Lips touch, she arches her back, moving even closer. He frees her breasts from the black negligée. A second kiss causes her to inhale slowly and distinctly. He feels her beating heart as distant artillery blasts increase its beat.

Never before has she allowed such reckless abandon with a man. A rush of passion flows as he gently spreads her shapely, now naked, body over the bed. He savors her soft and fragrant essence and her graceful body.

One overpowering need dominates and penetrates her heart and soul. He makes a suggestion in an American voice filled with desire. Elodie reacts with soft moans of acceptance and lifts her hips. Instinctually, he takes time to understand her as an unhurried, caring lover.

Energy and escapade come together. Fiery passion sends her blood pulsating through her body. She breathlessly speaks in French—inaudibly—no matter, he does not understand. She moans, expecting to explode when the relentless artillery shelling rattles the windowpanes. Aroused to near madness, she achieves a grand *crescendo*. Then tranquility...her heart returns to a normal beat. Now, a lovers embrace within the glow of a dying candle.

Elodie is confused by an awakening mind, unaware of the time except for rays of morning light filtering into the room. Wavering between fantasy and reality, she fixes her eyes on the very old ceiling beams. Perfectly still, her gaze consumes the recognizable bedchamber. Despite her beauty that easily attracts men, she is inexperienced in the art of lovemaking.

Church bells provide reality. Other church bells chime in, ringing in concert. She gets out of bed, walks to the windows and opens the drapes, allowing light to enter. The bells are consumed by deafening and incessant artillery in the distance—obscuring the distinction between the Western Front and the home front.

Elodie's evenings are forlorn, before she arrives beyond a dream. The night yields to the reality of another day of war. Another day at Hospital Number 8, where she is no stranger to despair. First, she must emerge from the fog of her erotic dreamscape. Gazing into the large mirror, she says aloud, "*Mon Dieu.*"

CHAPTER 74

MEUSE-ARGONNE

The First U.S. Army continues to move east on the Western Front, ever closer to Germany. With a victory at St. Mihiel, the American Army will advance with over 400,000 doughboys to the Meuse-Argonne.

The Meuse-Argonne region of France is heavily fortified with the Kaiser's army. The German defensive entrenchments with many divisions, heavy guns and artillery are considered to be impregnable. However, the allies have a decisive strategy to force a German retreat. Given the long line of German emplacements within complicated and uneven terrain, the men must "go over the top" to go on the offensive—and they will do so.

Hundreds of ally planes will bomb defensive positions to disrupt German reconnaissance, followed by an artillery barrage from thousands of guns. Then, the allies will advance between the Meuse River and the Argonne Forest, starting the largest battle ever engaged by the U.S. Army.

A key objective of the Americans and the French is to advance through a corridor leading to a railway. Capturing the railway would break a German support, supply and communication hub. As a result, the Germans would withdraw from France and the Kaiser's army forced to surrender. Centori is close to another rotation, but he waits for a confirmed pause in the action.

CHAPTER 75

RESIDUAL RESISTANCE

A light rain falls as Elodie goes into her bedchamber and turns down the bed. A welcomed night after another stressful day at Hospital No. 8. The Allied offensive at St. Mihiel has increased the exhausting work.

She slips into her bed and takes a book from her nightstand, an erotic book written by a French woman. Reading romance novels stirs her romantic fantasy for his touch on her open body. In the space of semi-consciousness, she generates a vivid dream world, creating her own fantasy where her desires are set free.

She takes a deep breath, slowly exhales and releases the pressure of the day. Turning to the comfort of the night, she will cast off the shackles of sexual repression and of the extreme stress of the day. Then, she drifts to sleep and enters her lucid dream. She is aware that she is dreaming and controls the players and the plot...

"Have I kept you waiting too long?" Elodie says.

"It seemed like an eternity," he says.

He takes the bottom of her dress and removes it from her raised arms. She takes the pins from her hair. Her shining hair falls to her neck in wild disarray. His hands move from her bare shoulders causing an emotional surge. He steps back to admire her entire figure, "You are beautiful, Elodie."

"You make me feel beautiful. I am born when you kiss me, die when you go to war...and live when you return."

Moving closer, he slides an arm around her waist and kisses her lips. She returns the kiss with greater intensiveness. Accepting the signal, he gently separates her legs. She offers no residual resistance and he touches the most intimate part of her body. A naked embrace arises and fuels their intense ardor. Any hesitation washes away in waves of sensation. With the eyes of a woman falling in love with a soldier, she declares, "Love me Adobe, love me now."

Soon after, Elodie's hips move in a wild rhythm launching her into his arms as strong sensations run through her body. Suddenly she cries out, releasing fiery desire. Vague war activities are audible, ever so close and eclipse the reconciliation within her body. Then, her book crashes down on the hard wood floor, ending her safe and vivid dream. Elodie wakes up alone, jolted from her fantasy and shaken by the glare of day. This time more comforted than disappointed. After all, she should not find him in bed.

Drifting in a sea of indifference, she is aware of looking out the window at the artillery flashes, but she is unaware of how long. Slow to focus, she reaffirms that she is an ardent French woman. Another night of dreams blurs the line between illusion and consciousness for Elodie.

Mon Dieu. He came to me again this night, she thinks. Then, *Elodie remembers that he will come to her today and prepares for the Café Cheri rendezvous.*

CHAPTER 76

CAFÉ CHERI - CHATEAU CHERI

At their favorite *Café Cheri* table, he sits across from her with the smell of coffee and croissants in the air.

"What's wrong?" Elodie asks.

"Why do you ask?"

"You seem troubled."

"Weary, I guess. Tired of this war and sick of the trenches, the barbed wire and craters. Destroyed buildings and landscapes are an all too familiar sight. Most of all, the dead and broken men. The miseries of a senseless slaughter. Dante could not have imagined this horror in his inferno."

"You are here with me now."

"Yes, of course," he says while remembering silver medallion. Yet, nothing in the Spanish-American war prepared Centori for the horrifying, apocalyptic battles of modern industrialized warfare. The Western Front is a forsaken frontier; nothing flourishes except death. The world had sunk into madness, embracing lunacy with open arms. Seemingly, the destruction of European civilization is the goal.

He continues, "This crazy world is at war with no wiser minds to stop the leaders. Beyond the mass killings, the dead soldiers look so horribly dead. At least those killed would not suffer old-age indignities," Centori rationalized with little conviction. "I am sorry. How are you?"

"I am fine," she answers also with little conviction.

They order a *café au lait*, a *café noir* and *pain au chocolat* before she provides a more accurate answer.

"We are stressed at the hospital, more than usual. The air raid warnings are increasing. Most of the time we are too busy to notice the screaming sirens."

"If the Germans sense that defeat is inevitable, they will stop at nothing. Are you close to an air raid shelter?"

"Close enough, I suppose."

"I noticed a poem by an English soldier, Wilfred Owen. He writes about the war. I have a copy of one that impressed me the most."

Elodie takes a sip of her *café au lait* and says, "You would like to recite it to me?"

Reaching into his tunic, he unfolds a paper and says, "It is short but powerful. I will let you read it for yourself." He hands her the paper and reaches for the *café noir*. She looks down and reads the poem titled, "Anthem for a Doomed Youth."

> What passing-bells for those who die as cattle?
> Only the monstrous anger of the guns. Only the
> stuttering rifles' rapid rattle can patter out their
> hasty orisons./ No mockeries now for them; no
> prayers nor bells, nor any voice of mourning save
> the choir—The shrill, demented choirs of wailing
> shells./ And bugles calling for them from sad
> shires./ What candles may be held to speed them
> all? Not in the hands of boys, but in their eyes
> shall shine the holy glimmers of good-byes./ The

pallor of girls' brows shall be their pall; their
flowers the tenderness of patient minds,/ And
each slow dusk a drawing-down of blinds.

Elodie's eyes are misty as she hands the poem back and says,
"His writing is emotional and spiritual about the horrible reality
we are facing."

"Yes, his expressions are passionate. I sense resentment and
commitment at the same time."

He puts away the paper and breaks the morose mood with,
"You haven't touched your *pain au chocolat*."

"I can say to same about you," she reacts with humor.

"Elodie, you admired my silver medallion."

"Yes, it is a beautiful work of art."

"I wear it for good luck."

"I see."

"It has brought me good luck. Meeting you was good luck."

"It is very special for representing an idea, not emotion."

Disappointed by her reaction, he tries again, "It was given
to me with great honor, I would never give it to another lightly,
you see."

"I understand, but it fascinates the eyes and the mind, not
the heart."

"Please accept it as a gift—from my heart."

With her opinion softening, she offers, "I am sorry; you are
too kind to offer such a gift. I just don't know what to say."

"Say yes, and accept it in the spirit it is given."

"Yes, I accept it and will wear it at all times and be close to
you at all times."

He gently places the Silver Medallian over her head, "Wear
this gift well, Elodie."

She smiles and softly says, "I love this medallion. I will wear it well."

***

They leave the café and stroll through streets lined with wine stores, antique shops and old bookstores. Elodie touches the silver medallion and smiles her approval. Although aimlessly walking, she seems to be aiming for her house. Her mind races to resolve conflicting feelings while her body shows the poise of a woman ignoring remaining resistance.

Once inside Elodie's house, Centori finds the atmosphere dramatically changed and thick with tension. She offers a glass of *Château Margaux*, wine of Bordeaux. He flashes a quick smile and she returns a strained smile. Taking in her expression, he offers a toast, "To victory!"

"*Viva La Francias*," she rejoins.

Wasting no time—they have so little time together—he lightly places his hands on her shoulders. Elodie gently pushes away, expressing her uncertainty. He smiles, hoping to calm her, and says, "Something has changed. You seem distant." He knows the reason.

"*Mon Cheri*, I will not forget. Will you remember?"

He attempts another embrace; she draws back this time with clear opposition. Her throat tightens; it is dry with second thoughts. Then within the whisper of her breath, she gasps, "I'm falling in love with you."

Emotions are unpredictable, especially now. During normal times, she may have shown more decorum, but it is not normal times. The world is at war. She will release her feelings provided the world does not end. Wistfulness drapes over her demeanor.

She nervously moistens her lips, collects her thoughts and asks, "Is our love real or is it part of a wartime need?"

"It is real."

She accepts his kiss and he whispers in a sincere voice, "I love you too."

Frozen for a moment, she responds, "I thought we had enough time, but not any longer. Time has run out. I will cherish the memories forever."

"You have changed me forever."

She feels tears welling and asks, "Just memories then?"

"I think about you most of the time."

"You think of our rendezvous and nothing more."

Tears streak Elodie's cheeks; she begins to talk rapidly in French. Centori cannot answer, unable to connect her meaning. After he tries a series of French words, he pleads, "Elodie, in English please."

They laugh, breaking the tense moment, but for only for a moment before she continues in English, "This war will end soon. It is only a matter of time before the Germans sit down and sign an armistice, and then you will go to back America—to New Mexico."

"Yes, Elodie, but you don't understand me— the war will end, but we do not have to end."

CHAPTER 77

BATTLE OF THE ARGONNE FOREST

September 26 - November 11, 1918

Now, Centori and his regiment are positioned near the Meuse River and the Argonne Forest in northeast France. It is the scene of the Battle of the Argonne Forest.

Centori meets with his company commanders, two of the companies are led by first lieutenants.

"The Argonne is probably the strongest German defenses we will ever face in this the major battle of the war," Centori says.

Captain MuCuloch adds, "They are close to their supply lines and well defended, but with our First Army and the French 4th Army attacking, the German trenches will break."

"That is exactly the plan," Centori confirms.

***

The opening salvo of the battle allows an Allied advance of three miles before the British 1st and 3rd Armies attack. After an uphill charge in the open, the U.S. 2nd Infantry Division captures the heavily defended high ground of Monfaucon.

This action forced the Germans to retreat from a position that commands the Champagne region. The following week, American Doughboys commanded the summit. At the same time, the British were driving in the north to turn the enemy flank, converging with the Americans to contain the Germans.

By the end of the month, the Allies gain eight miles as German resistance hardens. In addition, stalemate, attrition, logistical and communication problems stall the Americans within the German lines. Hence, Pershing, who divided the army into the First Army and the new Second Army, changed the U.S. centralized command structure.

On October 3, Germany and Austria send peace messages to the U.S. with Germany determined to keep eastern territories. On October 5, the last Hindenburg defense is broken. Ludendorff's message to Berlin that the war is lost shocks the politicians. American and French soldiers continue to force the Germans to retreat. The British and Belgians do the same in northern Flanders. By mid-October, the Germans are retreating along the Belgium coast and northeast France; the Belgian and British forces continue to advance.

German troop strength decreases, but they are able to slow down the Allied juggernaut—and by October 19, the Allies are close to the Dutch frontier. A German defeat seems inevitable.

Two days later, the 90th Division arrives on the line of the Meuse-Argonne front. Centori and all the Tough 'Ombres establish a good starting position for the next attack: cut off a pocket of Germans at Bois de Bantheville. The hard fighting of the Tough 'Ombres wins the battle. The success of the mission earns high commendations for the 90th Division.

Then, two companies of Centori's 358th Regiment cross the Andon Brook. Machine gun fire opens up stopping the men before artillery preparation cleans out the enemy. The Germans answer with a mustard gas attack, causing the evacuations of many doughboys. On the Verdun front, German counterattacks fail as the Tough 'Ombres hold their positions.

After steady German resistance for weeks, the Allies are able to break through the enemy lines. In the face of heavy casualties, the doughboys smash the German defenses. The advancing Allies find thousands of German soldiers willing to surrender.

On November 1, the Allied armies stop their juggernaut to regroup, and then the advance continues with attacks on German positons near the Meuse River. The Belgian and British armies move closer to Belgium while the U.S. First Army capture the last major German defensive line and hold the important Lille-Metz railroad.

As part of the final push, the 90th Division, on the right flank of the army, is ordered to capture a wooded ridge. The attack is a success. Other divisions are successful in breaking German resistance and forcing the Germans out of the Argonne.

In the end, one million American and French soldiers recaptured some 200 square miles. The Germans suffered 100,000 casualties; the Americans record 117,000 casualties. It is a high-priced victory, but it could be the final chapter of the war. The German leadership responds by reinforcing the Argonne front for a better negotiating positon in the coming armistice, showing no signs of surrender.

Doughboys of the First and Second Armies continued to attack German positions near the Meuse River. In addition, U.S. Army reinforcements advanced 20 miles before the armistice. With defeat certain, Germany requests a peace agreement.

On November 5, President Wilson told the Germans that peace discussions could begin with French Field Marshal Ferdinand Foch.

CHAPTER 78

ARMISTICE DAY

November 11, 1918

Major Adobe Centori arrives in Rouen at 8:00 a.m. The Allied Supreme Commander, Field Marshal Ferdinand Foch, and Allied and German generals meet today before 11:00 a.m. in the railroad car in Compiegne, France. An armistice will be signed to cease hostilities on the Western Front, finally ending the war.

The Great War will end today. Yet, the German high command continues hostilities in a way to gain better surrender terms. These last-ditch attacks on the Western Front will ensure that the war continues until the bitter end.

On this day, Centori rotated from the trenches to behind the lines—for another chance to see Elodie. What will he say to her now that the war is ending? What will that mean for their future together?

At least he will mark the historic Allied victory and defeat of Germany with Elodie. Then without explanation, he has an unclear premonition. Unable to find a car at the Rouen rail station, he begins the long walk to the hospital. Walking briskly from the rail station and past a row of automobiles painted olive drab, a gloomy feeling came over him. Assuredly, Elodie will be at work; assuredly, he is unaware of the aerial bombing of the Rouen hospital.

Unknown to Adobe Centori, German air raids attacked Rouen two days ago. Whether the *Deutsche Luftstreitkräfte*, equipped with machine guns, targeted a rear echelon hospital in the course of the bombing raid is unknown. German pilots may have miscalculated their range or headwinds or the altitude caused navigational problems. Perhaps the pilots relied on radio bearings and dropped bombs blindly that fell on the hospital. Whatever the case, General Hospital No. 8 was struck behind the lines, causing extensive alarm with material and psychological damage.

The aerial attack was unleashed at sundown and began with screaming blasts from machine guns. Then, bombs rained down; the explosions shook the entire area. The *Luftstreitkräfte* swept in from two directions and was helped by a dim moon, destroying large areas of the hospital and leaving sections in flames. On the ground, scores of people were killed and wounded. Additional casualties occurred when people hit by shrapnel from anti-aircraft fire stampeded into air raid shelters.

In the hospital, nurses helped the wounded and became targets of aircraft machine guns. Shots from low-flying planes shattered windows and bodies, destroying the lives of those helping others. Injured medical personnel and patients were powerless to seek shelter during the attack—many soldiers, doctors, nurses, and support staff are missing.

As Centori approaches the hospital, a feeling of gloom and then fear absorbs him. There are bomb craters in every direction within a scene of destruction. He hears batteries pounding in the distance. A short train of motor trucks rumbles past him, forcing mud over his puttees and boots. He sees an old man walking around the rubble. With urgency, Centori runs to the man and says, "*Monsieur, vous parlez anglais?*"

"*Non, seulement français,*" the man replies.

Without another word, he runs toward the hospital.

From two blocks away, devastation makes it difficult to find the hospital. He looks left and right—there it is—a view comes into focus. General Hospital No. 8, the largest base hospital in Rouen, is severely damaged with large sections in rubble.

Instantly, he breaks into a fast run, riveted ahead at an area that used to be an entrance. His doughboy hat flies off his head as he pivots to avoid a bomb crater. Soaked in sweat, he makes no effort to retrieve his hat as his heart crashes against his chest, pounding to the point of pain.

Terror takes hold of him as he runs toward what remains of the hospital. He stops at the foot of the rubble and frantically searches for anyone who could help or provide information, anyone who speaks English. He is alone. Then his spine goes cold.

Then, the morning sunlight reflects from a shining metal object. In a dazzling manner, the reflection captures his attention. He is drawn to the rubble that surrounds a shining object and shocking implication. His heart starts pounding. Shock takes possession of him; he frantically summons all his resolve. Absorbing the impact of the horror, he falls to his knees and releases a primal scream.

The brilliant dazzing reflection does not bring joy. Once a treasured possession, it is now a source of despair—no longer worn by the woman he loves. He pulls the Silver Medallion from the rubble and wails uncontrollably, repeating the words, "not again!" War created their love affair and war destroyed their love affair.

EPILOGUE

The Great War ended at 1100 hours, November 11, 1918. The impact and meaning of that historic event came gradually for most soldiers. When the selected hour struck, the highly unusual silence was an amazing surprise. After years of artillery and machine gun fire, the silence seemed strange. The American Army suffered 320,000 casualties with 53,402 battle deaths. The men of the 90th Division, having achieved their missions with distinction, earned an outstanding combat record. Intrepid commanders led courageous and dependable doughboys.

Under fire from August 20 to November 11, the 90th Division went over the top in two major operations with more than 7,500 casualties. General Pershing praised the division as one of the finest with commendations for action at St. Mihiel and the Argonne Forest.

It happened in a railroad dining car in the Compigne, France. Marshal Foch informed the Germans that captured land in Belgium, Luxembourg and France, and Alsace-Lorraine will revert accordingly. German armies must leave occupied lands and submit to an Allied occupation west of the Rhine. Scores of Navy ships and submarines must be surrendered along with heavy armaments. Naval blockades will continue and the Allies will seize thousands of trains and trucks. Dozens of additional conditions will be forced on Germany, including reparations for the war damage.

The German delegates were beaten and agreed to sign the armistice to take effect on the eleventh month, eleventh day and the eleventh hour of 1918. The extreme terms of the armistice would became intolerable to the German people, setting the stage for another war.

In 1919, Adobe Centori returned to the U.S. and eventually to his home in New Mexico. Circle C Ranch operations are conducted by Francisco Griegos, who had done so during Centori's service in France. War penetrates a psyche, creating powerful reactions, or no reaction. Centori has been slow to resume running the ranch.

On a cold March morning, three years after finding the Silver Medallion, Centori sits on Little Hill Top and watches the Cooper's hawks with intensity. He wonders if the birds are part of the world that shadows the death of millions of war victims, or part of another world.

Taking a shovel in hand, he digs a deep hole. Then, he reaches for a leather cloth. Burned into the leather is a Latin phase: *In coelo quies*. He removes the medallion from his neck, wraps it in the cloth and returns it to the ancient burial place.

Adoloreto "Adobe" Centori—Circle C Ranch owner—New Yorker, New Mexican, soldier, federal agent and friend, has never trusted happiness. He never did and he never will.

A coyote appears from nowhere. He turns to look into the coyote's eyes. A burst of sunlight causes the coyote to fade out of sight. Then, a face slowly fades in from the brightness. As the face comes clear, Centori's eyes open wide to welcome her.

***

The armistice would end on September 1, 1939 when Nazi Germany attacked the Republic of Poland starting the Second World War. On September 17, the Soviet Union invaded Poland. As a result, Germany and the Soviet Union annexed the defeated Poland as per the German-Soviet Frontier Treaty.

ACKNOWLEDGMENTS

Throughout the process of creating *Adobe Centori and the Silver Medallion* many friends and family have provided assistance. I am appreciative of their contributions. Thanks to Catherine Akel, Ph.D. and Nancy Maffucci, MBA for ongoing editorial support and for insights that have enhanced this story.

Also by
Daniel R. Cillis Ph.D.

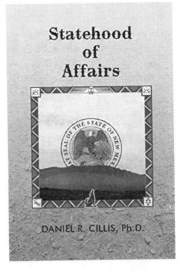

In 1911, New Mexico found itself at the center of an international conspiracy that threatened statehood. The unjust commitment of a woman to an insane asylum reveals a plot to find the missing Article X of the Treaty of Mesilla: the Revert Document. Tensions rise as the United States and Mexico are on a collision course. If the Revert Document emerges before Arizona and New Mexico attains statehood, Mexico could legally recover those lost territories thereby changing history. Affairs of the heart complicate affairs of state. Adobe Centori shares loves but different side of the border with Gabriella Zena—_La Guerrillera._

WATER DAMAGE

A TALE OF NEW MEXICO, NEW YORK, AND DAWNING TERROR IN AMERICA

Sequel to
Statehood of Affairs

Daniel R. Cillis, PhD

A horse-drawn wagon carrying a bomb loaded with dynamite and shrapnel explodes in front of the House of Morgan in New York. Dozens are killed, and hundreds are wounded in this Wall Street Explosion. Although New York and the financial center of the world recover, U.S. foreign policy will never be the same. In addition, attacks on U.S. munitions in New York Harbor and ship board explosions alarm the White House, the Bureau of Investigation and NYPD. This story continues the stories of Adobe Centori, Mad Mady Blaylock, Gabriella Zena and Jennifer Prower and tells the tale of Germany's secret war in America before the Great War.

In 1917, five years after New Mexico received its statehood, the United States entered World War I. With border tensions festering between Mexico and the United States, Germany attempted unsuccessfully to secure Mexico's allegiance with its Zimmermann Telegram. More than sixteen thousand New Mexicans joined the military, while civilians supported from the home front. Groups like the Knights of Columbus, YMCA and the Salvation Army, as well as Governor W.E. Lindsey's New Mexico Council of Defense, raised military funding. This book recounts the Land of Enchantment's influence on World War I from its beginning through to the 1918 Armistice.

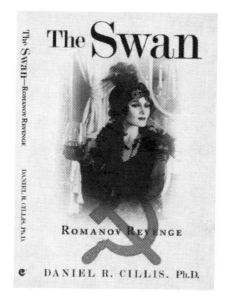

The Swan

ROMANOV REVENGE

DANIEL R. CILLIS. Ph.D.

During the Russian Civil War, that followed the Russian Revolutions of 1917, the royal family of Czar Nicholas II and Czarina Alexandra and their 5 children were arrested and executed. The killing of the Romanov family by the Ural Bolsheviks captured worldwide attention. Eventually, the story faded from widespread public mindfulness. Yet, one woman who was close to the family cannot forget the brutal slaughter.

04086940-00830971

Printed in the United States
by Baker & Taylor Publisher Services